Praise for Robert Asprin's MYTH series

"Stuffed with rowdy fun." —*The Philadelphia Inquirer*

"Give yourself the pleasure of working through the series. But not all at once; you'll wear out your funnybone." —*The Washington Times*

"All the MYTH books are hysterically funny." —*Analog*

"Breezy, pun-filled fantasy in the vein of Piers Anthony's Xanth series . . . A hilarious bit of froth and frolic." —*Library Journal*

"Asprin's major achievement as a writer—brisk pacing, wit and a keen satirical eye." —*Booklist*

"An excellent, lighthearted fantasy series."—*Epic Illustrated*

"Tension getting to you? Take an Asprin . . . His humor is broad and grows out of the fantasy world or dimensions in which his characters operate." —*Fantasy Review*

SOMETHING
M.Y.T.H. INC.

ROBERT ASPRIN

ACE BOOKS, NEW YORK

SOMETHING M.Y.T.H. INC.

An Ace Book / published by arrangement with
Starblaze Editions of The Donning Company/Publishers

PRINTING HISTORY
Meisha Merlin Publishing, Inc. edition / September 2002
Ace mass-market edition / August 2003

ISBN: 0-441-01083-0

ACE®
Ace Books are published by The Berkley Publishing Group,
a division of Penguin Group (USA) Inc.,
375 Hudson Street, New York, New York 10014.
ACE and the "A" design
are trademarks belonging to Penguin Group (USA) Inc.

PRINTED IN THE UNITED STATES OF AMERICA

10 9 8 7 6 5 4 3 2 1

This volume is dedicated to Eric Del Carlo

My new writing partner and friend who got me back on track as a writer by helping me remember that writing is fun and exciting, not an obligation to be discharged.

AUTHOR'S NOTE

For those of you who are encountering the Myth novels for the first time with this volume, it might be helpful if you peruse the "Who's Who and What's What" at the end of the book. It may help to make some sense(?) out of what's going on.

On the other hand, if you're one of those die-hard true fans who have been (sort of) patiently awaiting this volume since *Sweet Myth-Tery of Life* was first released in 1994, this is it. It's been eight years, and you're probably thinking of going back and re-reading that volume just to get back in stride.

Well, for me, it's been more like a seventeen-year haul, dating back to 1985, when I started writing *M.Y.T.H. Inc. Link*.

To elaborate, the first six *Myth* novels were written separately with contracts for one, one, two, and two books as the popularity of the series grew. Back then, fantasy/science fiction humor was not considered salable. (The *Myth* books, along with a LOT of help from Piers Anthony's *Xanth* novels, turned that around.) Anyway, originally the publishers were going to take a flier on ONE humor book. When it sold, they stretched to contract one more. Then two more. Then another two. Finally, in 1984–85, I was offered a six-book contract to continue the series. Of course, at the time, I was confident I could write two a year. (For more on that, see the Author's Note at the beginning of *M.Y.T.H. Inc. in Action*.)

More important, it gave me a "bigger canvas" to work with. That is, instead of having to come up with stories that would be resolved in one volume, or maybe have a few elements that would hang over into the next, I had six volumes to play with. As a result, there were story and character elements brought into book seven *(M.Y.T.H. Inc. Link)* as well as those volumes following that I was using to set up situations in later volumes.

The story for volumes eight *(Myth-Nomers and Im-Pervections)* through twelve (this one) was set up in volume seven *M.Y.T.H. Inc. Link*, and is actually one continuous story broken down into novel-sized segments. [Okay, *Myth-Ion Improbable* (book eleven) is a side trip, but that's explained in the foreword.] This current volume takes place, for the most part, concurrent with the events in *Sweet Myth-Tery of Life* (book ten) and it wraps up the whole Possiltum/Perv/Hemlock caper.

It also, after twelve volumes and twenty-three years of writing Aahz and Skeeve, is the last Myth novel under contract. I can't help seeing it as the end of one era and the beginning of another.

All in all, it's been a long haul. Hope you enjoy it and feel it's worth the wait.

Robert Lynn Asprin
February 2002

PROLOGUE

Like wildfire, word spread throughout the land—from town to village, from peddler to peasant—that their once-idyllic kingdom was now under the control of a mighty magician who held the queen in thrall.

Though it was customary for the common folk to pay little attention to who it was that ruled them, much less the antics and machinations of palace politics, this time it was different.

It was clear to even a casual observer that the magician dabbled in the Black Arts. He openly associated with and sought counsel from demons, who even now roamed the corridors of the palace. As further evidence of his other-worldly nature and preferences, the magician kept a fierce dragon as a pet . . . a rarity that even the animal-loving ecologists of the land found disquieting. For those who would scoff at the existence of magik and other super-natural powers, there were frightening rumors of another sort. It was said that the so-called magician was connected to the criminal underground, trading political influence for their assistance in keeping the populace under control.

Even considering all this, the people might have been willing to ignore the power shift, were it not for one thing . . . their taxes were being raised. While it was true that, even with the new increases, their taxes were barely half of what they had once been, the populace saw it as a grim foreboding of things to come. Once the magician succeeded in reversing the trend from lowering taxes to increasing them, it was asked, where would it stop?

Clearly, something would have to be done.

People who had never thought of themselves as heroes began to ponder and mutter, both singly and in groups, about ways to bring down the tyrant. Though they varied greatly in both skills and intelligence, the sheer volume of the plotters virtually insured the eventual downfall of the villain currently growing fat off the kingdom . . . the man they called Skeeve the Great.

ONE

If there is one thing that a background as a Mob rough-off artist does not prepare you for, it is conducting a democratic-type business meetin'.

Business meetin's in the Mob is usually conducted with as few participants as possible, to keep the potential witness count to a minimum, and the agenda consists of out-linin' a situation in as little detail as possible, and endin' with the simple instruction of "Handle it." Havin' to utilize one's people-type skills to obtain opinions and input from the other participants is as unlikely as havin' to conduct a press conference.

Still, this was the specific situational I found myself in, and was determined to do the best I could with what little trainin' I had.

"I assume there is some specific reason for this sum-moning."

That was Chumley talkin'. Even though he does a good job of playing dumb muscle when he's hired out as a troll,

when he isn't workin', he talks as good as anyone and
better than most.

"Ask Guido." Nunzio sez, jerkin' a thumb at me. "It's
his show."

Now Nunzio, in addition to bein' my cousin, is also
my usual workin' partner of choice. Unfortunately, as
sometimes happens even in the best of partnerships, we
happen to be in disagreement as to the necessity of this
meetin'. As the senior partner, I have pulled rank and the
meetin' is happenin'. As junior partner, however, Nunzio
is standing on his right to bein' a royal pain in the butt
while assistin' me.

"Well," I sez, ignoring Nunzio, "since we're all here,
we might as well get started."

"Just a minute, Guido. Aren't we missing someone?"

This is Aahz pipin' up from where he has been leanin'
against the wall next to the door. Him, I've been expectin'
trouble from.

I favor him with a level stare.

"If youse is referrin' to the Boss, Aahz, I am well aware
that he is not present. In fact, that is one of the reasons
for this meetin'. You see, certain information has come
to the attention of Nunzio and myself, and it is our . . .
my desire to consult with all of youse as to whether it is
wisest to pass said information along to the Boss, or if
we should simply act on it ourselves."

This is, of course, the crux of the disagreement between
Nunzio and myself, as, in the Mob, to hold a meetin'
without the participation or even the knowledge of one's
boss is to invite the interpretation that one is planning
some kind of takeover attempt. In the Mob, such activity
is justification for termination of the most permanent kind.

Now, knowin' the Boss the way we do, I do not fear
that this is a likely possibility. Particularly as we are tryin'
to figure out how to support him, not attemptin' any kind
of power play. The truth of it is, we is quite fond of the

Boss and have prospered individually since havin' been assigned to him.

Nunzio, on the other hand, maintains that the Boss is at least technically a Mob sub-chieftain, and that callin' this meetin' is therefore treadin' on even thinner ice than some of the capers we have taken part in since joinin' the Boss's crew. At least then, he sez, we could claim that we was actin' under orders from the Boss. This meetin' is definitely my own idea, and as such I will be held personally responsible for any fallout which might occur from it. There are times when bein' an order-takin' goon and therefore low on the chain of accountability has its advantages.

"Let him talk, Aahz. I, for one, want to hear what he has to say."

That is Massha talkin', earnin' her one of my widest smiles for her support, which she returns with a wink.

Aahz starts to say somethin', then just shrugs and gestures for me to start.

"Okay," I sez. "Now you all know that durin' our recent assignment to stop or curtail the expansionist type efforts of Queen Hemlock, Nunzio and me stood duty for a while as Army types. Well, it seems that Hugh Badaxe's scouts have uncovered some news that affects the Boss. Not wantin' to take official action or use official channels, he looked up one of the squad that was servin' under Nunzio and me and sent 'em here to pass the word along to us."

I turn and wave a hand at the figure lounging against the wall behind me.

"This is Spyder. I guess you'd call her an old Army buddy of mine. Spyder, I'd like you to tell the crew what you told Nunzio and me."

Now Spyder was probably the toughest member of our squad after Nunzio and me. She is whipcord lean with the grace of an alley cat and twice the attitude. Due to Army regulations, her short hair is now a uniform light brown instead of the rainbow of colors it was when she enlisted. This has not, however, made her look any the more military or otherwise domesticated. She continues to give the impression of bein' an over-aged gutter punk ready to fight and half-lookin' for it, which is exactly what she is.

She has been studyin' the assemblage as they came in like a store security type durin' the holidays. As I feed her the cue, like, she cranks her cat-eyes around to look at me direct.

"I don't think so," she sez, shakin' her head.

"Spyder," I sez, tryin' to keep my voice level. "This is not the time to get cute. I told you I wanted you to talk to these folks. Now tell them what Hugh Badaxe told you."

"You said you wanted me to talk to some friends of yours, Swatter," she snarls. "And I agreed. Didn't even say 'Boo' about us meeting in a stable. But who are these people? The big hairy guy with the different-sized eyes, and the two with the green scales and pointed ears? You can't tell me they're from around here. And unless I've gone completely around the bend, that is definitely a dragon listening in from that stall. I want to know whom I'm talking to before I open up. I know you and Nunzio, but these people . . . ?"

She shakes her head again and lapses into a sullen silence.

"What's with the 'Swatter' bit, Guido?" Massha asks.

"It's an old Army nick-name," I sez wavin' her off. My attention is focused on my cousin. "Nunzio, I thought you explained things to the squad back when we was hangin' together at Abdul's."

"You said to explain about Abdul being a Deveel," he sez with a shrug. "I told them that our work with the Boss had involved traveling to other worlds and dealing with strange creatures, and occasionally some of those creatures popped up here in our world. I also said that they could be tricky or nasty or both, and if any showed up, like Frumple, to let us handle them."

"That's it?" I sez. "You didn't tell 'em anything about dimension or dimension travelers?"

"At the time, that seemed more information than was necessary," he sez. "They accepted it."

I am findin' this hard to believe, especially as Nunzio is usually one who loves to go on endlessly about anything at the drop of a straight line.

"Well," I sez. "That was then and this is now. Perhaps you could elaborate a bit for Spyder's benefit, with particular attention to the players currently in the room."

"No problem," he sez, and turns to Spyder. "You see, those worlds I mentioned before are actually called dimensions. There are thousands of them out there, and the beings that live in them do so, for the most part, without any knowledge or awareness of the other dimensions' existence . . . except, perhaps, for occasional legends or folk tales. A few, however, are not only aware of other dimensions, but often travel back and forth between them either as part of their work or simply adventuring. These dimension travelers are generally referred to as 'demons' when they're in a dimension other than their own."

He paused and cocked his head at her, quizzical-like, but Spyder just keeps starin' at him.

"Now the group assembled here," he continues, "is known in some worlds as M.Y.T.H. Inc. We've joined together to provide services to individuals or groups who require assistance of an unusual nature or capacity. Our leader, or Chairman of the board, is the Boss . . . or, more commonly Skeeve. You know him or have heard of him as Skeeve the Great, currently serving as Royal Magician to the Court of Possiltum.

"The green, scaly gent with the impressive teeth and the dour expression is Aahz. He was Skeeve's main in-

structor in magik and things dimensional, and is currently
the boss's main advisor and second in command. He hails
from the dimension Perv, which makes him a Pervect, as
is his cousin, Pookie, the lean mean feminine version over
there, who has recently joined our ranks to assist Guido
and I with our bodyguarding duties."

Those two individuals incline their heads politely to
Spyder, who nods back.

"The large, hairy gentleman is Chumley. He and his
sister Tananda, who is currently covering our home office,
are from Trollia. As you might guess, he would be what
you might have heard referred to as a Troll."

Chumley gives Spyder a deep bow. I notice with some
approval how quickly Nunzio skips past the reference to
Tananda. She and Spyder met briefly on our last assignment, but Tananda was disguised at the time so Spyder
didn't spot her as a demon. The two of them didn't really
get along, as they were both interested in the same man,
so Nunzio is wise not to dwell on the subject.

"Last, but certainly not least, is Massha. As you can
see, it's hard to miss her, due both to her larger-than-life
size and her propensity for bright outfits and jewelry. She
and the Boss met on a caper in the dimension Jahk, and
she was impressed enough to sign on as his apprentice.
Within our crew, however, she's a full-fledged member."

"Hiya, Sugar!" Massha sez, wigglin' her fingers at Spyder. "Don't worry. We're not nearly as nasty as we look."

Spyder is so busy starin' at Massha she forgets to nod.
This is not surprising, as Massha is quite an eyeful. Nunzio's statement that she is 'larger than life' does not to
begin to encompass her stature. Massha is huge, in all
directions except up. What's more, her bright orange hair
and green lipstick are upstaged by her loud, flashy clothes
and enough jewelry to stock a small craft show.

"The other member of our troupe is Bunny, who isn't
with us at the moment because she's meeting with Skeeve

to go over the kingdom's finances. Like Guido and me, she's from this dimension, which is known elsewhere as Klah, incidentally, so there's nothing unusual about her appearance other than she's cute as a button." He notices Spyder makin' a face at this, so he adds, "It might also be worth noting that she is the niece of Don Bruce, the Fairy Godfather of the Mob locally. Speaking of which, you should also probably know that as far as Don Bruce is concerned, our whole operation is a part of the Mob. An independent, stand-alone part, but a part nonetheless."

"Gleep!"

"Oh yes," Nunzio sez, pointin' to the contributin' party. "The aforementioned dragon is Gleep. He is the Boss's pet and has assisted us on several capers, much to the dismay and demolition of our opponents. Does that satisfy your curiosity, Spyder?"

He has not bothered to include either himself or me in the introductions, since, as was earlier noted, we have worked with Spyder before during our brief hitch in the Army. Of course, our own appearance is no less memorable than the rest of the team. We both have the size and build of professional athletes of the contact sport variety, only more intimidatin'. This was pretty much a prerequisite in our earlier work as Mob collection specialists.

"I guess. At least, explains a few things," Spyder says comin' off the wall at last.

"Then, returnin' to the point of this meetin'," I sez, "could you now tell everyone what Hugh Badaxe asked you to pass along?"

"If you say so," she sez with a shrug. "Basically, General Badaxe has been getting reports that pockets of malcontents are forming in the kingdom. Right now they're small and mostly talking, but he's concerned that they might eventually try taking action. Specifically, armed, organized action."

"Pardon me, my dear," sez Chumley, "but I'm afraid

I'm missing something here. Why is Hugh having you tell us about this? If there's a possible rebellion shaping up, why doesn't he simply handle it with the Army?"

"I'm getting to that." Spyder waves. "You see, it's not the kingdom they're talking about overthrowing. It's the magician. The Great Skeeve. The Boss, as you call him."

"How's that again?"

Aahz is no longer leanin' against the wall, but standin' tall and looking very attentive.

"Well, it seems the word going around the kingdom is that an evil magician, that's Skeeve, has the Queen in thrall and is actually running the kingdom from behind the scenes," Spyder explains. "While most folks don't seem to care much one way or the other, there are those who are talking about trying to . . . how do they put it . . . free the kingdom from his merciless grasp."

"But that's patently absurd!" Chumley sez with a frown. "We all know Skeeve. He's got a good head on his shoulders and shows marked potential as a magician, but mostly he's an organizer. There isn't an evil bone in his body."

"I'll tell you something else, Missy," Massha puts in. "Skeeve is helping to bail out the kingdom at Queen Hemlock's personal request. She's the one who's trying to blackmail him into marrying her. How does that fit with your 'magician holding the Queen in thrall' scenario?"

For a second I am afraid that Spyder is going to go after Massha for the 'Missy' comment, but she doesn't. This is a good thing, as Massha not only outweighs her on a factor of five or six to one, but also packs a mean magikal wallop in some of the jewelry she wears.

"That's how you all see him," Spyder sez, "and I'm inclined to believe you, mostly because I trust the Swatter and Nunzio. You've got to look at it through outsider's eyes to understand what's going on.

"Skeeve definitely has the Queen's ear, that much you

admit. Then there's the rumor that he consorts with strange, otherworldly creatures." She pauses and looks pointedly around the room. "And some say he's guarded by a ferocious dragon." She nods toward Gleep, who cocks his head at her. "And, finally, there's persistent talk that he has underworld connections and is supported by local organized crime."

She pointedly does not look at Nunzio and me, but the message gets across.

"Not to offend the current company, but the citizens are thinking that 'If it walks like a duck and quacks like a duck . . .' " She lets the sentence trail off. "Anyway, whatever the truth is, that's what the talk is that's going around the kingdom. General Badaxe thought you should know."

I let the silence drag on for a few minutes as the team digests what they've heard.

"Thank you, Spyder," I sez at last. "I guess the big question, and the reason I called this meetin', is: What are we going to do about all this?"

"I think you were right, Guido." Aahz sez. "Both for calling the meeting and for thinking that it's best if Skeeve didn't hear about this."

"I'll have to second that," Chumley sez. "The lad's never been particularly good at handling women, and this thing with Queen Hemlock has him tied up in knots. I say let's look into this ourselves and let Skeeve focus on his other problems."

"Right," sez Aahz. "Particularly since this might get a bit messy, and Skeeve has always had a bit of a weak stomach when it comes to out-and-out violence, however necessary."

He looks around the assemblage, and receives a round of nods. I am glad to see him takin' command of the meetin', since this now gets me off the hook.

"Okay," he sez. "Here's how I see it. For the time being, I think most of us should hang tight here at the palace to keep an eye on Skeeve and be sure nobody tries a sneak attack or assassination. Guido, I think you and Nunzio should do some scouting to see exactly what the situation is and what we can do about it. Maybe you can figure out a way to rig it so Spyder here gets assigned to assist you."

So much for gettin' off the hook.

"I think I'd like to tag along on that as well, if nobody minds," Pookie sez, speakin' up for the first time.

"If you can handle the disguise spells so you don't scare the populace, I don't see why not," Aahz nods. "Okay. If everyone agrees and there's nothing else right now, I suggest we break this up and get back to what we were doing before Skeeve comes looking for us."

As the various players start to wander off, Aahz draws me to one side.

"Just one thing, Guido," he sez. "If you have to call another one of these meetings, I suggest you do it somewhere other than the stables. Skeeve has a habit of dropping by here from time to time to talk to his dragon."

I glance over at Gleep. Instead of his usual playin' around, he is sittin' very still and starin' off into the distance, just as if he were thinkin' hard about somethin'.

TWO

Our intrepid band of adventurers has raised an excellent point. To wit, who could possibly be upset enough with Skeeve to try to organize a resistance movement?

A quick glance around the kingdom (it's not that big a kingdom) yields the answer.

Open rebellion rarely if ever comes from the rich. Their weapon of choice is money (that's why they're rich) rather than swords and bows. What's more, they can afford to employ expert retainers to do their fighting for them. Of course, those skirmishes usually take place in court or with auditors rather than on the field of battle.

By similar logic, the poor are seldom the ones to stir up trouble. Frankly, they can't afford either the time or the money it takes. Peasants are kept too busy by the endless tasks involved in tending fields and livestock to meddle openly in politics, and even begging takes a surprising amount of time and energy just to raise sufficient coins for one or two days' worth of sustenance. As long as things don't deteriorate to a point where everyone is starving and they have nothing to lose, the poor don't really care much who's running things.

For real grumblers and agitators, one need only look to those who have some money, a bit of education, and too much leisure time . . . which is to say the middle class.

For an example of this, one need look no further than the annual gathering of the Sherwood Arms Bow Hunting Club. In happier times, this was simply a group of buddies who happened to live in the same suburb, specifically the Sherwood Arms, that scheduled their vacations at the same time so that they could all go bow hunting in the nearby Possiltum Royal Game Preserve. In truth, this time was usually spent drinking and playing cards while letting their beards grow out, all in the name of 'roughing it' . . . which in itself was no small achievement considering the rather primitive conditions prevalent in Possiltum at this time. This year, however, there was a markedly different air to the proceedings . . .

"I still don't get it," Tucker said, helping himself to some more wine. "Why do we have to do anything about this Skeeve character?"

"Haven't you been listening to Robb?" put in John, the broad-shouldered, construction-worker type of the group. "He's raising the taxes. You know who that's going to hit the hardest, don't you? Small businessmen like us."

"Speak for yourself, Johnny," Tucker snorted. He was the physical opposite of John, being rather short and rotund. "Unlike some, I wouldn't exactly call my business little . . . excuse me, small."

"Would you like to step outside and say that, Tuck?" John said, getting to his feet and straightening to his full, considerable height.

"Umm, Johnny? We are outside," Tucker said wearily, making no effort to match John's actions.

Even though they were good friends and neighbors, the 'big/little' thing was a sore spot between the two men. Tucker owned several franchises of the biggest fast-food chain in Possiltum, making him notably more successful than John, whose third attempt at starting a company, this one renting porta-potties, was still struggling for life.

"Could you two knock it off for a while?" said Robb impatiently. "This is important."

"Sorry, Robb," John said, sinking back into a sitting position. "It's just that the Cholesterol King here gets under my skin from time to time."

"It's just that some of us have the sense to give the people what they want . . . like ready-cooked food," Tucker sniffed. "Why try to rent porta-potties in a country where most folks' idea of a toilet is the nearest tree or bush?"

"For the same reason some people don't eat at your grease holes," John shot back. "They appreciate sanitation."

"Sanitation, is it?" Tucker snarled. "Well, let me tell you . . ."

"ENOUGH!!" Robb interrupted. "Do you want to hear this or not?"

The two combatants sank into a sullen silence, shooting each other occasional dark glances. Even though Robb did not have John's height and muscles, there was an intensity about him that made him the automatic leader of the group.

"Now, the part that really worries me," Robb continued, "is that not only is this Skeeve character raising the taxes, he's diverting part of the army to collect back taxes as well. Tell me that doesn't affect all of us."

The group exchanged uncomfortable looks. While all of them filed their taxes on a regular basis to avoid penalties and interest, they had gotten in the habit of relying on the kingdom's laxness in collecting monies owed. As a result, they all had sizable sums owed in back taxes, which could be disastrous if said sums were to be forcibly collected all at once.

"Okay. I'll admit that could be bad," said the well-dressed, red-headed member leaning against a tree. Slender to the point of being waspish, he nonetheless habitually carried himself with a poise and dignity that forbade anyone from even thinking of him as 'Red.' "So what are we supposed to do about it?"

Robb craned his neck and looked around before he spoke, as if expecting to find a spy or a soldier lurking behind a nearby bush.

"I've got a plan," he said, lowering his voice. "The way I have it figured is that we can pay our taxes like good citizens, then steal it back from the collectors after they leave."

"That's illegal," the red-head said. "If we got caught, my law practice would go right down the toilet . . . no offense, John. I don't like taxes any more than anyone else, but I can't see becoming a hoodlum over it."

"Don't give me your legalistics, Will . . . and don't call me a hood," said Robb. "At worst, we'd be outlaws. For that matter, we're already outside the law. We've been poaching in the Royal Game Preserve for years now."

"Nobody cares about that," Will said. "Rodrick wasn't into hunting the way his father was, and Hemlock has been too busy expanding the borders to bother with minor domestic crimes. If we start messing with the tax collectors, though, somebody's going to be upset."

"Besides, how long has it been since any of us have actually shot anything on one of these jaunts?" Tucker muttered.

"Like we could hit something if we tried," John agreed. Despite their claims to being a bow-hunting club, the group, without exception, were incredibly bad shots with a bow and arrow.

"What's the rest of it, Robb?"

That was Allie speaking for the first time. As someone who was trying to make it as a stand-up comic and merely renting a room in John's house, he was not really a full-fledged member of the crew, but they kept him around for laughs.

"How's that again, Allie?" Robb said, innocently.

"C'mon, Robb," Allie said. "Don't try to kid a kidder. I've gotten to know you pretty well. Taxes and back taxes are one thing, something everyone can agree on. If I know you, though, there's something else. Something's bothering you. It's big enough to have you thinking about taking on the army, even small units of it, but it isn't so big that you can use it as a sales point to the rest of us. I'm just kind of curious as to what that something is."

All eyes turned to Robb.

"Okay," he said with a sigh. "I've heard that one of the things Skeeve is thinking of doing is wiping out the Royal Game Preserve. It's been proposed to him that he can raise money for the kingdom if he lets the lumber companies level the forest, then sell the land to developers."

"Where'd you hear that from?" said Tucker.

"From my niece, Marian. She works part time as a maid at the castle."

"A maid? Named Marian?" John said thoughtfully.

"Forget it, Johnny," Robb waved. "Between her job and her schoolwork she hasn't got any time to be a part of this."

"I'm missing something here," said Will. "Since we don't really do any hunting, why should it matter to us if they level the Preserve?"

"Think about it. All of you," Robb said. "The preserve and our hunting are the only excuse we have for these yearly outings. If it goes away, so does our excuse for getting out of the house. How many of you would really rather spend that time with your families?"

A thoughtful silence descended of the assembly. Despite their personal differences, the one thing that united the men was that they were all married. Happily married, of course, but it's been said that a man can only take so much happiness without a break.

"So, Robb," Tucker said, breaking the silence. "Tell us more about this plan of yours."

Of course, for hotbeds of sedition and revolution, one need look no further than institutes of higher education. Rampant idealism untempered by the practicalities of having to earn a living is great for producing droves of untested youths who are convinced they know how to run the world better than those currently in charge.

It has been noted, however, that the atmosphere at these centers tends to go through cycles, penduluming from radical to conservative and back again. At the time of our tale, the schools are in a conservative loop, so only one group of misfits figures into the current equation.

The particular group under study is a gaggle of students who periodically gather to play a popular Fantasy Role-Playing game. For those of you unfamiliar with this pastime, this is a game where people get together, often dressed up in medieval garb, to assume the role of various fantasy characters in order to act out (usually verbally) a scenario devised by the game master. The fact that games of this sort are extremely popular in Possiltum might be explained by the fact that such costumes are very easily obtained here, and at incredibly low cost.

•   •   •

"I tell you we simply can't let this opportunity pass us by!" ranted Storm (known in her everyday life as Wilhemia). An imposing, hefty young woman, she was the group's main rule-citer and enforcer, and wasn't used to being argued with. "A chance like this only happens once in a lifetime, and then only if you're lucky."

"Frankly, I'm not wild about our chances," said Egor, also known as Melvin. A pale, fey, math major, he rarely strayed from his books other than to take part in these gaming sessions. Surprisingly, he had proven to be the only one who could vaguely hold his own in disputes with Storm.

"Are you kidding? An evil sorcerer holding the kingdom in thrall?" Storm shot back. "It's the exact type of situation that we've been practicing how to handle for months."

"Reality check!" said Egor, holding up a hand. "What we've been doing is playing around with make-believe characters in pretend situations. You're talking about going up against a real sorcerer with real guards. Guards, I might add, who carry real weapons that inflict real wounds. Not the kind that you can heal up with a die roll, the kind that can make you real dead. What's more, from all reports, the opposition has been doing this professionally for years, not months. Like I said before, I don't like our chances."

"I'm not talking about us trying to attack him head on, you dufus," said Storm.

"Oh?"

"Of course not. I'm not stupid."

"I stand corrected on both misconceptions," Egor smiled, bowing slightly from his seat.

Storm stuck her tongue out at him.

"So what exactly is it that you're proposing?" said Red Blade, a bespectacled, skinny drink of water known more commonly as Herbie, who tended to think of himself as a warrior trapped in an academic's body.

"I think we should do what it says in the book," Storm said grandly. "I think we should form a Fellowship."

"Book? What book?" frowned Red Blade.

"What book? What book?" mimicked Storm. "*The* book, of course. C'mon, Red Blade. How many books are there that center around a Fellowship?"

"Oh. *That* book." Red Blade said.

[Author's Note: The reader may be wondering how this and occasional(?) other anachronistic references appear in Possiltum. Early in the series, it was established that Deveels are merchants extraordinare and make a large portion of their money buying and selling new inventions through the dimensions, which is why broadswords, chain mail, and crossbows seem to appear anywhere fantasy is written. Similarly, they will pirate literary and musical works and market them through the dimensions without regard to copyrights or royalty payments. You know, kind of like the Internet.]

"As I recall," said Egor, "there was quite an array of characters in that book. Where do you expect to find their equivalent here in Possiltum?"

"It's not as hard as you think," Storm said. "Like, remember when we tried an FRP camp out last year?"

"I remember most of us getting poison ivy."

"Well, the guy who came up and told us that we couldn't have open fires in the park was dating Melissa for a while, and she still knows how to get in touch with him. I figure he'll do for a Ranger."

"Stretching," Egor said, hesitantly. "But keep going."

"Now then, for a dwarf . . . how about whats-his-name? PeeWee?"

"Now that's cold," interrupted Egor. "I mean, he's

short, all right, but I don't think he'll like you calling him a dwarf."

"We don't tell him he's a dwarf, silly," said Storm. "We just invite him along and let anyone who sees us draw their own conclusions."

"Hmmm. We'll hold judgement on that one. What else?"

"Okay, and as far as kismet goes, my roommate's brother enlisted in the Army as a sorcerer, and it happens that he's in town on leave with a couple of his buddies. I figure we can recruit them just by saying we're lining them up with some blind dates."

"Cute idea," said Egor, "but I don't think they'll go along with helping us attack the sorcerer. Last thing I heard, he was in kind of tight with the army."

"Like I told you before, we aren't going to attack him directly," Storm said. "Remember the book. We're going to do an end run and try to knock out his power source."

"And exactly how do you propose that we do that?"

"Are you ready for this?" Storm said, her eyes gleaming. "Everybody gather around."

She produced a small box from her belt pouch, and opened it with a dramatic flourish. Nestled inside was a disembodied finger with a gaudy ring embedded in its flesh.

"I think I'm going to be sick," Red Blade said weakly.

"What in the world is that, Storm? And where did you get it?" demanded Egor.

"From Marian," said Storm. "You know, the one who works part-time at the castle? She swiped this right out of the sorcerer's room and passed it to me."

Everyone looked alternately at the ring and each other.

"So what are we supposed to do now?"

"Well, I've got to try to come up with an elf," said Storm confidently. "I need the rest of you to spread out and see what you can do about finding a volcano."

•   •   •

If there's anything with greater potential but less actual usefulness to society than a college student, it's a recent graduate who has yet to find gainful employment and is thus still living with his or her parents. Thus it is with a particular only son of the wealthiest land developer and landlord in Possiltum . . .

"I gotta say, Donnie, of all the hare-brained schemes you've come up with, this has got to be the craziest!'

"C'mon, 'Nardo," the youth said to his heavyset companion. "It'll be a snap. Trust me on this one."

Viewed at a distance, the duo would appear not unlike a staid and somber owl being circled by a scrawny but energetic jay . . . or, more accurately, a popinjay.

"Trust has nothin' to do with it," Nardo said. "I didn't keep bailin' you out of one mess after another all the way through college to let you end up gettin' chopped up by some army types."

Like many rich fathers with only one offspring, Don's father was phobic about anything happening to his heir apparent. One of his solutions had been to hire Bernardo as a manservant/bodyguard for his son when shipping him off to school. While a close bond had sprung up between the two, in many ways closer than the bond between father and son, Bernardo never lost sight of what his main job was . . . or who was paying the bills.

"But I can't just stand by and watch while this sorcerer gouges the heart out of my father and his tenants with higher taxes," Don insisted.

"As near as I can tell," Bernardo said drily, "what he's doin' is savin' the kingdom. Queen Hemlock had lowered the taxes way too far to be able to keep things on an even keel. The economics were all wrong."

"How did you figure that?" Don asked, genuinely puzzled.

"By stayin' awake and listenin' in all those classes you slept through," Bernardo said. "Bodyguards can't sleep on the job. Besides, it came in handy when I had to sit in for you on some of those tests."

"Well, whatever." Don shrugged. "That's still going to be a sizable hunk of change the tax collectors will be moving around. I should be able to shake some of it loose."

"This wouldn't have anything to do with your father cutting off your allowance until you find a job, would it?" Bernardo said suspiciously.

"It's just a way of picking up a little expense money to tide me over until I get settled," Don protested. "It's not easy to find an appropriate position for someone of my talents."

"You can say that again," Bernardo muttered.

"What was that?"

"Nothin'," the manservant said innocently. "The thing is, Donnie, even if you can get past the army types, I'm not sure you want to mess around with this Skeeve guy. I've heard rumors that he's connected, and that could mean big trouble."

Bernardo spoke with no small amount of knowledge on that score. He had worked for the Mob once before retiring and getting hired for his current position.

"Oh yeah. Sure." Don laughed. "I've heard that he keeps a dragon, too. Tell me, have you seen a lot of dragons around?"

"Well . . ."

"I tell you it's all just hoopla to scare people into letting him have his way. As for me, I'll believe it when I see it."

"I've seen some things I still don't believe," Bernardo sighed.

"There. We're in agreement!" Don beamed.

Bernardo stared at him for a moment, then played his trump card.

"If your father gets wind of this, he'll throw a fit," he pointed out. "Then he'll take it out on me."

"I've got that all figured out," Don said, excitedly. "I'll do it under a secret identity. I'll use another name, so no one will know it's me."

"Oh, that'll fool 'em big time," Bernardo said, pointedly eyeing his charge's colorful costume. Don had always prided himself on standing out in a crowd, and today was no different.

"Of course, I'll wear a disguise, too," Don added. "I tell you, I have this all worked out."

Bernardo sighed heavily and shook his head. Despite his certainty that this latest venture was doomed from the onset, he also knew it was next to impossible to change Don's mind once it was set on a venture. Especially if that venture involved a new wardrobe.

"So tell me," he said, "what name have you picked?"

"Well," said Don, "I'm small, but I'm strong and stubborn. I was thinking I'd call myself El Burro."

"I suppose it's better than 'Jackass,' " Bernardo muttered.

"What?"

"Nothin'. And the outfit you have in mind?"

"I haven't completely made up my mind there," Don admitted. "Maybe something in a brown suede jumpsuit with fur trim and accents."

"Oh that will blend right in with a crowd," Bernardo said, rolling his eyes. "Why not go all the way and wear shiny black . . . with boots, gloves, and a cape?"

"Hey! I like that!" Don grinned.

"Donnie, I was kidding!" Bernard said desperately.

"I wasn't."

THREE

Regardless of the impression youse may have gotten about the disregard Nunzio and me have of laws and rules, there are certain lines which we do not cross on a regular basis. One of these is lyin' to the Boss. We may omit certain details from our reports, but this is done more to spare him any discomfort. An out-and-out lie is something we both try to avoid like the plague. This is, in part, because bein' caught in a lie within the Mob does not involve perjury charges, but a much more violent and permanent fine.

As such, I am not wild about havin' to get the Boss's permission for this new assignment without really lettin' him know what was goin' on. Such a task would require subtlety and finesse, two qualities I am not often called upon to resort to in my work.

Realizin', however, that it was something that had to be done, and that, as the one who proposed this whole venture in the first place, it fell to me to do it, I applied myself to the problem as best I could. With Nunzio's help,

I came up with a story that should stand up under all but the closest cross-examination, then had Chumley coach me on preparin' the necessary scroll for a hand prop.

Finally, convinced that I was as prepared as I could be with the amount of time available, I knocked on the Boss's door.

"Say, Boss. Can you spare a minute?" I sez, pokin' my head in.

The Boss was sittin' at his desk with a goblet of wine in his hand and a full pitcher nearby.

"Sure, Guido. Come on in. Pour yourself some wine."

It seemed to me it was awfully early in the day for the Boss to be hittin' the vino so hard, but figured it was none of my business. When it came right down to it, I had little idea what the Boss had to do on a day-to-day basis while tryin' to straighten out the kingdom's finances or what kind of pressures it put on him. What he did and how he did it was up to him.

"I never drink when I'm workin', Boss," I sez, "but thanks anyway. I just need to talk to you about something."

I glanced around and pulled up a chair. Now that I was here, I wasn't sure quite how to start.

The Boss seemed to realize this, and leaned forward with a slight smile on his face.

"So, what can I do for you?" he sez, friendly-like.

I took a deep breath and plunged in.

"Well, Boss, It's like this. I was thinkin' . . . You know how Nunzio and me spent some time in the army here?"

"Yes, I heard about that," he sez with a nod.

"Bein' on the inside like that, I get the feelin' I probably know a little more'n you do about the army types and how they think. The truth is, I'm a little worried about how they're gonna handle bein' tax collectors. Know what I mean?"

I paused and looked at him expectantly.

"Not really," he sez, with a bit of a frown.

This was not goin' as well as I hoped, but I pressed on gamely.

"What I mean is, when you're a soldier, you don't have to worry much about how popular you are with the enemy, 'cause mostly you're tryin' to make him dead and you don't expect him to like it. It's different doin' collection work, whether it's protection money or taxes, which is of course just a different kind of protection racket. Ya gotta be more diplomatic 'cause you're gonna have to deal with the same people over and over again. These army types might be aces when it comes to takin' real estate away from a rival operation, but I'm not sure how good they are at knowin' when to be gentle with civilian types. Get my drift?"

The Boss was noddin' now, which I was glad to see.

"I hadn't really thought about it, but I see your point."

More confident now, I moved on to the next point in my plan.

"Well, you know I don't care much for meddlin' in management type decisions," I sez, "but I have a suggestion. I was thinkin' you could maybe appoint someone from the army to specifically inspect and investigate the collectin' process. You know, to be sure the army types don't get too carried away with their new duties."

The Boss is frownin' again.

"Um . . . I don't quite understand, Guido. Isn't it kind of pointless to have someone from the army watching over the army? I mean, what's to say our inspector will be any different from the one's he's supposed to be policing?"

"Two things," I sez with a smile. "First, I have someone specific in mind for the inspector . . . one of my old army buddies. Believe me, Boss, this person is not particularly fond or tolerant of the way the army does things. As a matter of fact, I've already had the papers drawn up to formalize the assignment. All you gotta do is sign 'em."

I hand him the scroll I've been carryin', which he un-rolls and scans.

"Funny name for a soldier," he sez, half to himself. "Spyder."

"Trust me, Boss," I sez. "This is the person for the job."

Instead of signin' the scroll, the Boss leans back and looks at me hard-like.

"You said there were two things," he sez. "What's the other?"

"Well, I thought you could have a couple of envoys tag along," I sez, casual-like. "You know, reportin' directly to you. That way you could be doubly sure the army wasn't hidin' anything from you."

The Boss stares at me in silence for a few beats before he responds.

"I see," he sez at last. "And I suppose you have a couple specific people in mind for the envoys as well?"

This catches me by surprise. His question is well in advance of when I had planned to raise this point, and I have to scramble a bit mentally to re-arrange my carefully prepared script.

"Um . . . As a matter of fact . . ."

"I don't know, Guido," he sez, shakin' his head. "I mean, it's a good idea, but I'm not sure I can spare both you and Nunzio. If nothing else, I want Nunzio to do a little work with Gleep. I want to find out if there's any-thing wrong with him."

We are now on the same page again, and I relax a bit. If this is the Boss's only problem with the proposal, I'm home free.

"Ah . . . Actually, Boss," I sez, carefully, "I wasn't thinkin' of Nunzio. I was thinkin' maybe Pookie and I could handle it."

Nunzio and I had talked this out. Upon reflection, it didn't seem like such a good idea to have all three of the

Boss's bodyguards away from him at the same time. In addition, it made sense for one of us that was familiar with the Boss's habits to stay with him, while the other teamed with Pookie. Now, I've been a bit taken with Pookie since she first knocked me flat, so when Nunzio suggested that he be the one to stay behind, I didn't argue much.

The Boss seemed genuinely surprised by this suggestion, however, so I hurried on.

"Really, Boss," I sez. "There ain't a whole lot to do here for three bodyguards. I mean, the way I see it, the only one here in the castle who might want to do you any harm is the Queen herself, and I don't think you have to worry about her until after you've made up your mind on the marriage thing. I was just lookin' for a way that we can earn our keep . . . something useful to do."

For some reason, this seems to make up his mind for him, and he reaches for a quill.

"Okay, Guido," he sez, signin' the scroll. "You've got it. Just be sure to keep me posted as to what's going on."

That touches a bit of a nerve, as it is exactly what we don't intend to do.

"Thanks, Boss," I sez, gatherin' up the scroll while avoidin' direct eye contact. "You won't regret this."

With that, I make my getaway, which is to say I leave the room.

Pausin' in the corridor outside, I realize my heart is beatin' at a vastly accelerated rate for someone who has simply been conversin' with his employer. It occurs to me that I am lookin' forward to bein' out in the field again, as my normal rough-and-tumble pastimes seem to be far less stressful than this diplomacy stuff.

FOUR

It is a well known fact that events do not always follow anticipated plans when occurring. This is particularly obvious to one in my own chosen line of work, as it is the main reason that a peace lovin' individual such as myself finds it necessary to stock what has become known as 'tools of the trade,' which is to say an assortment of blunt and not-so-blunt instruments. Ninety percent of the situations requirin' violence occur when things do not go as planned and priorities shift from profitability to survival.

But I digress.

I had figured that the biggest difficulty involved with our sub-rosa scoutin' mission would be gettin' the Boss to go along with it without actually lettin' him know what we was doin'. As it turned out, this was very easily accomplished, partially because he was distracted tryin' to figure out what to do about the kingdom's finances, and partially because he had started drinkin' early that day . . . somethin' which seems to go hand in glove with workin' with numbers. In any case, with a minimum of verbal

duckin' and weavin', I emerged with a scroll reassignin'
Spyder as Royal Investigator and his approval for Pookie
and me to tag along as his personal envoys. Piece of cake.

As to the actual scoutin', I figured it would literally be
a walk in the country. A stroll around the kingdom away
from hassles and jealousies of the palace and court. Un-
fortuitously, as Nunzio is so fond of pointin' out to me,
I am not the swiftest or most detail-oriented person when
it comes to such calculations.

What I had overlooked in my assessment of this assignment was who I would be workin' with: to wit, Spyder and Pookie.

Now, I must hasten to qualify that by sayin' that I have
nothin' against either of these two. I've always had a soft
spot for Spyder since our days in the Army when she kept
mouthin' off to the Drill Instructor who was easily three
times her size, taking the best he could dish out in the
way of backlash, and still keep givin' him attitude. (Okay.
So it wasn't real smart, but it showed a never-say-die
spirit that is not all that easy to find these days.) As for
Pookie, everything I've seen about her marks her as a
seasoned pro, starting with our first meetin' when she
knocked me cold but didn't kill me when she thought I
was attackin' the boss.

All of which is to say that I like Spyder and I respect
Pookie. As such, it never occurred to me that there would
be any problem with the three of us workin' together as
a team. I still maintain my reasonin' was correct as far as
it went. The factor that I didn't take into consideration
was that we had set up a team consistin' of one male,
which was me, and two females . . . both of whom had
what might be politely referred to as 'highly competitive
natures.'

This oversight rapidly became apparent soon after our
tour had started. We had stopped for our first rest break,
which was really Spyder and me restin' while Pookie

roamed on ahead a little "to look things over."

"So tell me, Swatter," Spyder sez, starin' after Pookie, "why is it we need three people for this scouting mission?"

Now, right away I don't like the sounds of this, but decide to play it straight at least for the beginnin'. I mean, on the off chance Spyder is on the level, it is part of the duty of the old guard to help the newcomers gain experience by answerin' their questions so's they don't have to learn everything by trial and error.

"The main reason is that there's safety in numbers," I sez. "Seein' as how we are not sure how many of the opposition there may be, much less who they are or what level of skill or arms they might have, we have a better chance of dissuadin' them from doin' anything foolish with a substantial show of strength on our side. What is more, should we fail in said dissuadin', that same strength increases our odds of survivin' said foolishness once they commence the doin'."

"I'm not quite sure I got that," she sez.

I sigh, realizin' once more that a goodly percentage of the population does not share my command of the language.

"Simply put, three of us will make anyone think long and hard about jumping us . . . and if they do, we can probably make them wish they hadn't."

"Oh. Got it," she sez.

She lapses into silence for a while, and I congratulate myself on my abilities as a teacher.

"But why her?" Spyder continues suddenly.

"Excuse me?" I sez, momentarily caught off guard in midself-congratulatin'.

"You have a fairly good-sized crew back there at the palace," she sez. "Why did you have to insist on dragging along the lizard lady? For that matter, you and I could probably handle things on by ourselves."

Now, I have a clear recollection of Spyder bein' at the meetin' when Pookie volunteered to come along with us, but no memory at all of my insistin' on that point. Rather than arguin' this, however, I decide to cut to the chase and go after the main issue at hand.

"Why, Spyder, I am surprised at you," I sez, shakin' my head. "For a minute there you sounded just like a jealous female."

"It isn't that, Swatter . . . well, not entirely," she sez. "It's just that having someone else along is like saying that you don't think I'm good enough to cover your back. And then when you make it her . . . I guess it's hard for me not to take it personally."

"Now I want you to listen to this close," I sez sternly, " 'cause I do not want to have to go over it again. You are a good kid, Spyder, and I have liked you since the first day we met in boot camp. You are tougher than any three army types I have met, exceptin' maybe me and Nunzio when we was in, and I would never worry if you was coverin' my back. You're smart, and you got great potential and a good future at whatever you decide to apply yourself to. In contrast, though, Pookie is a professional. She has made her decision and already done her developin'. What is more, from what I've learned about Pervects like her and Aahz, she's been a professional for longer than you've been alive. She is good at what she does, and we are lucky to have her along on this caper. Don't let the professional respect I have for her detract from your knowledge of the affection and admiration I hold for you. Instead of sulkin' and feelin' bad, you should be takin' advantage of this chance to watch her in action. You can maybe learn a few things, which is what I am hopin' to do myself."

At this, Spyder sort of grunts and pulls into herself. I am not completely able to ascertain if this is because she is considerin' my words or merely sulkin'. In part, this is because Pookie has reappeared and I am slightly distracted watching as she approaches us.

As she promised back at the palace, Pookie has changed her appearance by the use of a disguise spell so she will not upset or frighten the local populace, most of whom are not used to seein' a demon strollin' down the road. To this end, she has replaced her normal green scales, yellow eyes, and pointed ears with skin and hair similar to those of us who normally dwell in this dimension. That, however, is as far as she has gone with her disguise.

What she has not changed is the fact that she is noticeably a female type. I had considered suggestin' to her that she might be less noticeable and more authoritative if she had disguised herself as a male type, but upon further consideration felt that it might be detrimental to my continued good health to attempt to argue the male/female thing with her.

Further addin' to her current image is that she has retained her normal workin' clothes, which for her consists of a sort of skin-tight leather jump suit with assorted straps and slash pockets for carryin' her arsenal. Not only does this outfit fail to hide the above-mentioned fact that she is female, it also clearly marks her as someone who is not normally from these parts.

Last but not least, the disguise spell has done nothing to change the way she moves. Now if this latter piece of information does not mean anything to you, then you have never spent any time in a profession or situation wherein your survival depends on an accurate appraisal of the violence potential of those comin' toward you before the actual action starts. For most people, movin' consists of little more than puttin' one foot in front of the other. In this manner, they manage to propel themselves from place to place without fallin' over, but that is about the extent of it. Trained athletes and those such as myself who have developed their muscles for use beyond normal walk-a-day necessities are more smooth and balanced when they move, but still tend to be a bit on the heavy-footed side. Pookie is one of the rare types that do not move so much as they glide. Not only are they always balanced, but each gesture and movement flows into the next like it is some dance that only they hear the music to. When you see someone who moves in this manner, as pleasing as it is to the eye, I strongly advise that you do not enter into a hassle-type confrontation with them, for they are likely able to tag you three hits to your one and from directions you did not consider possible to be hit from. Movin' as she does, it is clear to me that, disguise spell or no, Pookie will not exactly blend into the crowd wherever we go.

As I said, however, it is pleasin' to the eye (professionally speakin', of course) and I allow myself this pleasure as she walks up and plops down next to me.

"So, have you managed to settle things with your little girlfriend?" she sez, shooting a glance over at Spyder's back, as that individual has chosen to walk away as Pookie approached.

Now havin' just played this scene with Spyder, I am in no mood to treat such banter lightly.

"Pookie," I sez, "meanin' no disrespect to your age, the exact numbers of which you have not chosen to share, I must ask if you can still recall bein' young?"

This earns me a sideways glance and a pause before she responds.

"It's a stretch," she sez, "but I think I have some dim recollection of those days."

"In that case," I sez, "you might recall how it was when you was first getting started in the rough-and-tumble business. However cocky you might have been at the time, there was always a strong undercurrent of insecurity. The funny thing was, even more than wonderin' how you would match up against the opposition when the crunch went down, you was worried about fittin' in with those who were on your own side. To my estimation, that is what is goin' on with our young colleague over there."

"Hmm. Interesting point," Pookie sez, nodding slowly. "You know, Guido, you're a lot more sensitive and perceptive than you let on."

"To answer your question, however," I sez, ignorin' the compliment as I have never been good at acceptin' them, "Spyder did ask me about your role in our expedition. What I told her was that rather than viewin' you as a rival, that she would be better off puttin' her jealousies and insecurities aside and learnin' from you, as you are obviously a professional who would never let such things affect your actions or judgments."

"Ouch," Pookie sez with a grimace. "Okay, Guido. You've made your point. I'll pull in my claws and take the little darling under my wing . . . to mix a metaphor."

"Good," I sez. "That will probably make this caper much easier on all of us."

"Speaking of that," Pookie sez, "can you give me a bit more input as to exactly what it is we're doing? I've been in a lot of different kinds of action, but a tax investigator or a royal envoy is a new one to me."

"Actually," I sez, "this is not a bad time for us to go over that together. Hey, Spyder!"

When she looks over, I beckon for her to join us.

"We were just talkin' about how this might be a good time to go over how we are goin' to approach this caper," I explain.

"Now, as I see it, we are supposed to be checkin' out what, if any, plots are bein' hatched against the Boss and either neutralize them or report back to the team to plan some counter-measures."

"That's the plan as I understand it," Spyder sez with a shrug. "Since most of the rumors we've gotten have come from the Army types who have been reassigned as tax collectors, we're going to try to intercept them at one of their rendezvous points and interview them to find out exactly what's going on. Depending on what we hear, we'll make our plans from there."

"Right," I sez. "The rendezvous point we are headin' for right now is the one for the tax teams workin' the population centers closest to the palace. The theory there bein' that those areas pose the most immediate-type threat to the Boss."

"Okay. I understand all that," Pookie sez. "I guess my question is, how do we play it? Are we the velvet glove or the iron fist?"

"That is indeed going to be the tricky part," I sez. "On the one hand we want to put a stop to any foolishness which might be in the makin', but on the other hand we have got to be careful that we do not inadvertently stir up more trouble than we are quellin'. Again, we will just have to wait and see who and what it is we are up against."

"Well, we aren't going to find out sitting around here," Spyder sez. "I guess it's time for us to get moving again. Ummm . . . Pookie? Can I talk with you for a bit? I've got some questions about your disguise spell."

"Sure, kid," Pookie sez. "Whatever you want to know."

I wait for a while, curious about what it is they are goin' to say, but then I realize they are both starin' at me. Takin' the hint, I get up and start along the trail again. They give me a bit of a lead, then follow along, just out of earshot.

As much as I had encouraged them both to talk to each other, I find this arrangement to be a bit annoyin', as it leaves me with no one to talk to except myself. Then, as the sound of both of them laughin' reaches me, I begin to contemplate which is worse: Travelin' with two women who do not get along, or travelin' with two women who do.

FIVE

I am forced to admit that the balance of our journey to the rendezvous point was one of the more interestin' trips I have ever partaken of.

Most of this arose from Spyder's interest in Pookie's disguise spellin' abilities. This interest took the form not only of questions as to the extent and limitations of said spell, but numerous requests for demonstrations of the same.

From what I managed to overhear, it seems that much of Spyder's personality evolved as a direct result of her appearance. That is to say, she was always a skinny tomboy type that no one took seriously as a girl. Bein' faced with such overwhelmin' evidence that she had no chance to compete in the feminine games, she naturally took up the tough-babe mannerisms as it was the only outlet for her previously mentioned competitive streak. Now, already well into her formative years, all that had changed with her discovery of disguise spells.

As we made our way along, Pookie showed off her

magical prowess by providin' Spyder with a seeming endless array of different body types and outfits . . . "new
looks," as she referred to them. What is more, each new
look included a certain amount of coachin' as to how to
move and act to make said look believable. This provided
them both with hours of amusement as they huddled and
giggled together, happy as a pair of defendants in front
of a bought jury. Spyder was havin' the time of her life
playin' at bein' various types of broads, and Pookie was
takin' advantage of a rare opportunity to play dress-up
with a real live doll.

I myself did not take part in these festivities. In fact,
any effort on my part to offer input or opinions was firmly
discouraged, rejected by a series of glares and eye-rollin's
along with various snorts and murmured comments in
which "men" seemed to be the main derogatory word em-
ployed.

Even though, as everyone knows, I am a sensitive soul
who enjoys social-type interaction, this exclusion does not
bother me over much. In fact after a while, it becomes
rather enjoyable watchin' the two of them at play.

For one thing, as I have noted before, neither one of
them is particularly hard on the eyes, especially not in
some of the outfits that Pookie is tryin' on Spyder, most
of which display considerably more of her anatomy than
has previously been my privilege to view.

Then, too, I have other things with which to occupy
my mind. You see, with all this contemplative time at my
disposal, I have been able to consider from many angles
the situational into which we are walkin'. While, despite
my considerable experience on the subject, I do not pretend to know women as well as women do, on the other
hand, I do know men.

What we are effectively going to do when we reach the
rendezvous is to walk in on a pack of workin' men and
assert ourselves as authority types, requirin' that they ex-

plain themselves and their actions to us for our analysis and approval. This in itself is not a situation designed to endear ourselves to the individuals under examination, as they tend to automatically resent any outsider tryin' to tell them how to do their jobs. On top of this, the main authority type, our Royal Investigator, is a female type who is currently workin' overtime learnin' how to be cute and cuddly.

Now, I am not one who refuses or resents havin' to accept female types in authority roles, and I do not defend those backward thinkin' members of my gender who do. The actualities of the world, however, require the acknowledgement that those types do exist, and, from my observations during my limited time in the ranks, seem to make up a majority of the Army types like those we are on our way to question.

Takin' all this into consideration, I am devotin' the majority of my attention as we travel to stretchin' and preppin' my muscles, as well as updatin' the maintenance on my travelin' weaponry, honin' and oilin' as necessary. As I have noted before, a large part of bein' a peace-lovin' individual consists of bein' willin' and able to quash any trouble as soon as it starts, if not a little before.

When we arrives at the rendezvous, we all experience some surprise to find that we are the only ones there. That is to say, Pookie and Spyder are surprised that the Army types is not present, while I am surprised that they are surprised. Judgin' from my own limited military-type service, which Spyder was a part of, when assigned to some lame duty like garrison or tax collection and in the absence of any officer-types, it is unlikely at best that any soldier worth his or her salt will remain at the barracks or bivouac if there is anything at all more interestin' in the immediate vicinity.

In our case, it had been a dubious establishment called Abdul's Sushi Bar and Bait Shop. With minimal searchin' and inquirin', we discovered the hangout of the Army types we was supposed to be redezvousin' with. It was a bedraggled-lookin' place called the Tiki Lounge, which was decorated on the outside with dead brush and carved logs in a half-hearted effort to give it the appearance of a grass hut. To my practiced eye, it was obvious that some fire inspector's palm had been heavily greased to have approved something that gave every appearance of bein' a bonfire waitin' for the first torch. I also notices that the place has very few windows, and that the ones it does have are painted over black.

"Um, maybe we should wait until it's dark," I sez.

"What for?" Pookie sez.

"Oh, just a thought," I sez.

"Well," sez Spyder, startin' for the door, "I don't see any reason why we shouldn't get started right now."

"Just a second," I sez, shuttin' my right eye and holdin' my hand flat against it. "I think I got something in my eye."

They fidgets a bit, but wait sort of patiently while I counts to a hundred.

"Okay. Let's go," I sez at last, still holdin' my hand against my eye. "After you, ladies."

I hold the door for them as they enter, then follow them in. As I do, I drop my hand, open my right eye and close the left one.

This is, of course, an old trick. When movin' from a light area to a dark one, it takes a few moments for the eyes to adjust to the change in light. Those few moments can be extremely dangerous if there are potential hostiles in the area you are enterin' whose eyes are already accustomed to that lighting condition. To counter this, it is wise, if one has the time, to allow one eye, preferably one's dominant shootin' eye, to pre-adjust prior to makin' one's entrance. It may only make a little difference, but sometimes that small difference can save one's life.

Anyway, I slides inside and step sideways (so's I won't be silhouetted by the door before it closes) and scopes the place out. It is dark, as the painted-over windows had indicated, lit only by candles flickerin' on the low tables on the main floor and along the bar. There is a small group of locals clustered around a table in the corner, but I pay them little attention. Instead, I focuses on the dozen or so Army types hangin' on the bar and sprawled at nearby tables.

As near as I can tell, they is all low-level rankers without an officer or even a non-com amongst them. This also means they are relaxed and happy as only off-duty army types can be. It looks like they was all talkin' and drinkin' and playin' cards before we came in, which is to say simply enjoyin' each other's company. That was before we came in. Now, to a man, they are all focused on Spyder.

Remember how I mentioned that Pookie had been experimentin' with changin' Spyder's looks by usin' her disguise spell? Well, at the moment the outfit Spyder is wearin' bears only a passin' resemblance to the army's normal uniform. I believe I described said uniform back when Nunzio and me signed on for our brief stint in the Army, but for those of youse who have short memories, or, perhaps, have neglected to purchase that particular volume, I will reiterate. Basically, you have a short-sleeved flannel nightshirt, covered by a breastplate and skirt made of hardened leather, said skirt consistin' of multiple strips hangin' down from the waist. Sandals, a helmet, and a short sword complete the ensemble. All in all, it is designed to take an average wimp or pot-bellied draftee and make them look like a formidable fightin' machine.

This is, of course, not how it looks on Spyder.

First off, the flannel nightshirt has disappeared completely. The skirt is now noticeably shorter, like about halfway up her thighs, and is riding precariously on her hips rather than snug around her waist. Just in case this latter adaptation escapes the notice, it is emphasized by a noticeable reduction in the breastplate to a point where it not only leaves a wide stretch of her midsection exposed, it is barely large enough to qualify for its name.

The overall effect would qualify her for the centerfold of an Army-type magazine . . . if they had such things in this dimension. All she'd need would be a staple in her navel.

There is several long beats of utter silence as the room drinks in this vision. Then Spyder breaks the spell by openin' her mouth.

"Could you gentlemen direct me to the person in charge?" she purrs in a husky, tuck-me-in voice.

"Well, I'll tell you, Sweetheart," sez one brawny individual sprawled at a nearby table. "The Sarge isn't here right now, but if you want to wait for him, you can sit on my lap."

He gives a big, exaggerated wink to the other Army types in the room, who respond by eruptin' in guffaws and wolf whistles.

Spyder starts to turn red, which to those of us who know her definitely does not mean she is gettin' embarrassed. Rather, it is clear that we is about one step short of a full-blown donnybrook.

Unfortunately, someone thinks it is a good idea to take that step. One of the Army types sittin' directly behind Spyder decided to get cute by liftin' up the back of her skirt to try to peek under it.

Now, disguise spell or not, what's under it is still Spyder. Instead of givin' out a girlish squeal or tryin' to hold her skirt down, she simply pivots around and nails the guy with an overhand power punch. His seated position puts him lower than her, so she gets her full weight behind the hit with a bit of torque from a hip twist for a bonus. He goes down, not over the back of his chair but with it crumplin' under him, and doesn't twitch.

The laughter stops like a popped balloon as the rest of the Army types gape at their fallen buddy.

"Spyder, dear," sez Pookie, easin' forward, "what did I tell you about how a lady acts?"

"He was asking for it," Spyder growls, still hot under the collar.

"True enough," Pookie sez. "But, you see . . ."

Without lookin', she comes down with her left hand on the back of an occupied chair, dumpin' the soldier sittin' there on his back. At the same time, her right comes up behind the back of the head of the guy sittin' next to him, slammin' his forehead onto the table. Without a break in her movement, she leans across the table to the other two Army types sittin' there and slaps their heads together hard enough that their eyes cross and they slide to the floor.

". . . you can handle situations like this without breaking into a sweat," she finishes. "Needless exertion is not the mark of a real lady."

"I see," Spyder sez, noddin' slowly. "Thanks for the tip, Pookie."

It would be nice if that was enough to settle things, but by my calculations, that was only five out of twelve down, leavin' seven still in good condition. What's more, the survivors were no longer in a playful mood. They are slowly gettin' to their feet with blood in their eyes.

I figure it is about time I took a hand before things get serious and someone get hurt.

"Atten-HUT!!" I barks in my best parade ground voice and kick the door behind me open.

Now if there's one thing the Army drills into its recruits startin' in Basic, it's how to hit the position of 'attention' at any given moment . . . like if an officer type walks into the room. The Army types still on their feet immediately stiffen into said position, and even the ones still on the floor go a little more rigid.

This tableau holds for several moments, then someone sneaks a peek to try to figure out why they are called upon to perform in such a manner during what is obviously their off time. What he sees is me silhouetted in the doorway with one of my hand-sized crossbows cocked and loaded.

"As you were," I sez with a wide smile.

Of course, catchin' 'em all with such an easy trick does nothin' toward improvin' their mood.

"Real cute, fellah," one of them sez, turnin' toward me. "You want a piece of this action?"

"Just an interested observer," I sez, still hangin' onto the crossbow. "I would suggest, however, that before you go any further it might be wise to examine the young lady's orders. Particularly notice who signed them."

"I don't care if they're signed by Queen Hemlock herself," the guy spits. "We've got some payback coming."

"Close, but not quite," I sez. "We're not talkin' the Queen. She's under orders from the Great Skeeve."

"The magician?" he sez, swallowin' hard.

"That's the only Skeeve that I know," I sez with a shrug. "Now that you're aware of the real situation, however, if you want to keep playing around with his personally appointed Investigator, I figure that's up to you."

With that I fold my arms and lean against the door frame, a study of casual disinterest if I do say so myself.

"Nice speech, Guido," comes a voice from directly behind me, makin' me jump slightly. "Good to see you haven't lost your delicate touch in handling the troops."

I turns around to discover Sergeant Smiley, my old Drill Instructor, grinnin' at me.

SIX

"So, Guido. What have you been doing with yourself lately?" Sergeant Smiley sez. "I was hearing good things about you after you left basic."

"You did?" I sez, surprised.

"Sure. I always try to keep track of my boys after they leave training. My ladies, too." He gives a small bow towards Spyder without standin' up.

We is all sittin' around a table at the same Tiki Lounge, except now it has been cleared of Army types except for the Sergeant and Spyder.

"Anyway," he sez, "I heard you got a couple fast promotions, then you dropped out of sight. Some scuttlebutt said you were pulled for Officer's Training. Other rumors had you on special assignment to the Royal Palace. Now I find you all decked out in civvies tagging along with a Special Investigator. All in all, you seem to be doing pretty well for yourself."

Now, even though I kinda liked Sergeant Smiley, I did not feel inclined to tell him the whole truth, particularly under the current circumstances which is to say not under oath. While we were sort of old Army buddies, I was not sure how long that relationship would last if it came to light that I had been in the Army specifically to mess it up so that it would stop advancin' so fast while we figured out how to stop Queen Hemlock permanently.

"Can't complain," I sez carefully. "How about yourself? The last time I saw you, you were whippin' recruits into shape."

"It's the new reorganization thing," he sez with a sigh. "Now that we aren't on wartime footing, there's no need to recruit and train new soldiers. In fact, what with the cutbacks, we're hard-pressed to figure out what to do with the ones we have. I've got enough years in that I got to pick and choose when it came to re-assignment, so I went with what looked like easy duty with the new tax collecting unit."

He pauses to take a sip of his drink and makes a face.

"Easy duty. Yeah, right. It's like an open season on tax collectors, and we can't even get to shoot back because they're Possiltum citizens."

"Could you, perhaps, elucidate that a little?" I sez.

"I could," sez Smiley, "but I'll admit I'm curious as to why you're so interested."

I thinks for a few, then give a shrug.

"I don't think it's supposed to be a secret or nothin'," I sez. "There have been some rumors back at the castle that there may be a rebellion-type uprisin' in the makin'. We have therefore been sent out to check it out and report back as to how serious it is. Since it seems you have essentially been in the front lines when encounterin' signs of unrest, any input you can give us would not only be greatly appreciated, it would help us immensely in our investigatin'."

"That makes sense." Smiley nods.

"It does?" sez Spyder, but Pookie gives her a nudge and she shuts up.

"For the most part," Smiley sez, missin' the byplay, "it's just been some shouting and maybe a little produce tossing. Nothing particularly out of the normal, considering the popularity of tax collectors. The ones that get to me are the bozos who are actually holding up the collection squads."

"Let's start there," I sez. "I notice that you have referred to them in the plural, which would indicate to me more than one. In your opinion, is this an indication of an organized uprisin'?"

"I don't think so," Smiley sez, narrowin' his eyes in thought. "As near as I can tell, it's two separate groups operating independently of each other."

"Could you elaborate a little?" Pookie sez. "Someone of your military expertise couldn't help but notice details that would prove invaluable in our efforts."

Now Smiley is as vulnerable as any guy to bein' flattered by a doll, and he puffs up like a toad.

"Well, as I say, it would seem to be two independent groups," he sez. "That's based on the fact that they are operating in different locations and have two distinctly different methods of operation.

"There's one group that operates in and around the Royal Game Preserve. What they do is stay out of sight back in the underbrush. They launch a flight of arrows over the heads of the collection squad to prove that they're well within bow shot, then call out for the squad to leave the money and keep moving. It's interesting that they haven't actually hit anyone yet, but the threat alone is enough for the boys to surrender up the money and back away."

"They don't put up any kind of a fight? They just leave the money?" Spyder sez.

Smiley makes a face.

"You've got to understand," he sez. "Our standing orders are not to fire on the civilian populace. Remember that this is an internal assignment, not front-line work where any opposition is clearly enemy action. These are the civilians we're supposed to be protecting, and the brass doesn't want any incidents that could stir up the locals against the Army."

He takes another sip of his drink, then shakes his head.

"I'll be honest with you, though. Even if we weren't under orders not to fight, I'm not sure we could catch these guys. The woods are pretty thick and stretch a long way. What's more, it's their home turf, which gives them a big advantage. If they outnumbered us, they could keep picking us off from hiding and we wouldn't stand a chance. If we had them outnumbered, they could just melt away into the brush and we'd never catch them."

"With terrain goes the victory," Pookie murmurs.

"That's right," Smiley sez. "Say. It sounds like you know a bit about military tactics yourself."

"You said there were two groups," I sez, quick-like to distract him from askin' too much about Pookie's background. "What about the other group?"

"The other one's a real clown," Smiley sez, gettin' back to the subject. "It's only one guy, and he's dressed all in black, complete with a mask and a cape. What he does is pop up in the road ahead of the squad, waving a sword around and demanding that they surrender up the money and move on or suffer his wrath."

"Suffer his wrath?" I sez.

"That's what he says." Smiley nods. "Word for word. I couldn't make us something like that."

"Wait a minute," Spyder sez. "You're saying that an entire squad backs down from one guy with a sword?"

"It's a bit more than that," Smiley sez, sternly. "The guy in black does all the talking, but he's got a backup with him as well. Any time we've seen this joker, there's another guy standing in the background. He's a big guy, almost as big as you, Swatter. More important, he's got a crossbow, a custom job, trained on the squad and makes it real apparent that anyone who doesn't go along with the gag isn't going to make it back to the barracks."

"But there's only one shot in a crossbow, compared to how many in a squad?" Spyder sez.

"Uh-huh," Smiley sez. "The problem is, no one is particularly eager to be on the receiving end of that one shot. Also, remember that we're under orders not to fight with the civilians."

"That's convenient," Spyder mutters.

"Tell me more about that custom crossbow," I sez before Smiley can go after Spyder.

"That's easy," Smiley sez. "Without looking at them close up or actually handling them, I'd say it's almost identical to that mini crossbow you were waving at the boys when I came in."

Now to say that I found that tidbit of information particularly intriguin' would be more than a little understatin'. You see, both Nunzio and myself get our crossbows exclusively from a guy named Iolo, who is the finest crossbow maker I've met. While I've heard he does some work for Renaissance Fair people and some of the Medieval recreation types, the bulk of his production is bought up by people like us, which is to say those associated with or connected to the Mob.

"Could you give us some specific information as to where each of these two groups is workin'?" I sez, changin' the subject.

"I can do better than that," Smiley sez, finishin' his drink and gettin' to his feet. "I've got some maps in my tent. Come along and I'll show you, and maybe buy you a drink."

• • •

As our intrepid band of investigators leave the Tiki
Lounge, let us linger for a moment to witness what occurs
immediately upon their departure . . .

For several long moments after the investigators leave
with the sergeant, the group of civilians who were sitting
unnoticed at the corner table remain motionless and silent.

Finally, one of them speaks.

"It's all clear now, Bee. They've gone now."

The air shimmers around three of the assemblage, then
subsides, leaving their appearance changed, but still un-
remarkable.

"That was close," says one rather muscular fellow.

"You can say that again, Hy," says the man next to
him, their appearance marking them as brothers if not
twins. "Nice work with the spell, Bee. But I do wish you
had told us that the Swatter was on the other side of this
little caper."

"I didn't know myself," Bee protests, drawing himself
up to his full insignificant height. "I was told we only had
to dodge the Army, and last thing I heard, he and Nunzio
had resigned."

"Whatever," Shu says, giving his brother an elbow in
the ribs. "Now that we know, maybe we should rethink
this whole thing."

"Wait a minute," Storm says, leaning into the conversation. "What's going on here? Why are you guys so
spooked all of a sudden? Who was that goon, anyway?"

"That was the Swatter," Hyram Flie says. "Or Guido,
to use his real name. He and his cousin Nunzio were in
Basic Training with us back when we first enlisted. In
fact, he was our squad leader."

"To say he's a heavy hitter would be an understatement," supplied his brother Shubert. "He took both of us
to one side and gave us a lesson in manners the first day
we were in."

"He's also deadly with that crossbow," Bee says. "He

helped me qualify, which was a good thing or else I'd probably still be in Basic."

"So he was better than the other raw recruits," says Egor. "So what? You all got better with training, didn't you?"

"You don't understand," says Hy, shaking his head. "He and Nunzio were better when they first signed on than any of us will ever be."

"That sergeant he was talking to?" Shu says. "Well, he was our Drill Instructor. He got into it one time with Guido, and the Swatter took out both him and his corporal without even raising a sweat."

"Wait a minute," says Egor. "I thought the Army had rules against that kind of thing. Didn't he get into trouble?"

"They called it a training accident," says Hy with a grimace. "As a matter of fact, he got a promotion out of it."

"Did you see who he had with him?" Bee says. "Wasn't that Spyder?"

"If it was, she's changed her look," says Hy.

"Unless they were using a disguise spell for some reason," says Shu.

"Spyder?" says Storm.

"Another one from our old squad," says Hy. "Pound for pound, one of the nastiest scrappers I've run into. Mean as a snake and twice as fast."

"Yeah. That was a heck of a punch she used to flatten her admirer when they first came in," Egor says shaking his head.

"I think you're watching the wrong hand there," Red Blade says, speaking up for the first time. "How about the babe that took out four of them without blinking?"

"Another one of your old playmates?" says Storm.

"Never saw her before," says Hy.

"Good," says Storm. "I was starting to think we were in the middle of a reunion here."

"Even without seeing her in action," says Shu, "if she's hanging with Guido, she's probably a top-notch professional. I sure shouldn't want to go up against her."

"Which brings us back to our original point," says Hy. "Now that we've know that the Swatter and friends are in the game, do we stick around or head for the hills?"

"But you can't leave!" Red Blade says. "You agreed to help us!"

"We agreed to sit in on this conclave, mostly because it sounded like a good way for a couple of soldiers on leave to meet some girls," Hy says. "I don't remember agreeing to lock horns with a couple heavyweight widow-makers. That's not a party. That's suicide."

"Boys, boys," Storm says, holding up her hands. "Nothing's changed just because there are a couple extra hitters wandering around. Remember the whole idea of this plan is that we don't directly go up against anybody. They're looking for whoever is hassling the tax collectors, and that isn't us. Now let's have a couple drinks and talk about this calmly."

"Drinks are good," Bee says. "Okay. Who's having what?"

"Same as the last time," Shu says, glancing at his brother.

"Blood! Blood and raw meat!" says the elf from his corner.

"I told you before, they don't serve that stuff here," Hy growls. "Where did you find this guy, anyway, Storm?"

"Ordered him from the Complete Elfquest Catalog," Storm says. "Cut him some slack. He doesn't come cheap."

"I still want to know where you're going to find a dwarf," says PeeWee. "Right now, I'm the shortest one in the whole crew."

There was a tactful moment of silence from the rest of the fellowship.

"And, of course, another Volcano," Bee says wearily.

Truth to tell, that was the reason they were using the Tiki Lounge as their base of operation. Despite extensive research and inquiries, the only volcano they had been able to find in the entire kingdom of Possiltum, even with its expanded borders, was the specialty drink that was served here during Happy Hour.

They waited for their drinks to arrive; then, with great ceremony and solemnity unwrapped their prized ring, complete with severed finger, and dropped it into the flaming drink.

Nothing happened. Again.

Just like nothing had happened the last dozen times they tried it.

Also, like the last dozen times, no one was interested in actually drinking the Volcano after the ring and finger were reclaimed.

SEVEN

After bein' briefed by Sergeant Smiley and maybe havin' a couple more drinks for old times' sake, we holed up for a war council to decide what our next move should be. Two hours later, we was still councilin'. If you deduces from this that things was not goin' smoothly, you would be absolutely correct.

"And I'm sayin' that our mission is finished and we should report back to the Royal Palace," I sez, gettin' a bit testy.

We had been havin' this argument since about five sentences into the meetin', with neither side givin' ground. This is, in itself, sayin' somethin', as I was holdin' down one side of the argument by myself, while Spyder and Pookie were united against me.

"We're supposed to be scouting out potential centers of rebellion," Pookie sez. "Until we've looked into it first hand, all we have is rumor. We could have done that back sitting on our butts back at the palace."

"We've had an in-depth briefin' from the Army types

who have been experiencin' it all first-hand," I sez. "In their opinion, there is no organized rebellion. Just a couple small groups rippin' off the tax collectors. Now we have to report that back to the Boss and see what he thinks we should do next. Whatever else he is, Skeeve is still my Boss both in M.Y.T.H. Inc. and in the Mob. One thing I've learned over the years is the secret to a long and prosperous career, not to mention an extended lifespan, is to not get carried away with independent action by tryin' to second-guess what the Boss wants you to do."

"But we aren't taking independent action," Pookie sez. "We're just going to scout out the situation, which is what he told us to do in the first place."

"Hang on, Pookie," Spyder sez, steppin' between us. "Talk to me, Swatter. What's really bothering you?"

"Like I've been sayin'. The Boss . . ."

"I know what you've been *saying*," Spyder interrupts. "I also know you. Back in Basic, you pretty much ran the Bug Squad right under the nose of the Drill Instructor. When we got assigned to garrison duty and then the supply depot, you were still running things, and doing an excellent job of it. I know you can operate independently without playing 'mother-may-I' waiting for specific orders. So how come all of a sudden you're dragging your feet? There's got to be more to it than the chain of command. Heck, this whole expedition was your idea. So tell us what's eating you and quit trying to hide behind procedures."

The trouble was, she was dead-on right. I don't mind stretchin' the facts or obscurin' the truth a bit in front of a jury or even, occasionally, my colleagues, but I hate gettin' caught at it.

I rubbed my jaw while I thought things through, then decided to come clean.

"Okay, I'll admit it," I sez. "I'm pretty good when it comes to the rough and tumble stuff, but I'm a specialist.

Nearly all of the work I've done has been in cities and towns workin' against other individuals or gangs that are tryin' to avoid public attention. That's the kind of work I do. That's the kind of work I've trained for. The idea of wanderin' around the woods tryin' to run down opposition of an undisclosed number and strength that know the territory like we don't and aren't adverse to shootin' from hidin' leaves me cold. In that situation, we'll be as much out of our depth as the country bumpkins are when they come into the big city."

"What you're trying to say is that you're scared," Spyder sez.

I start to draw myself up to my considerable height, then just give a little shrug instead.

"Okay. If that's what you want to think, I'm scared," I sez. "That doesn't change the circumstantials of the situation."

"Pull in your claws, Spyder dear," Pookie sez, comin' to my defense. "Guido isn't scared; he's being a professional. Unlike some of the wannabe toughs you may have encountered in the past, Guido is the genuine article. He *is* tough, so he doesn't have to work at trying to prove it . . . even when provoked."

Now I knew that, but it was nice to hear Pookie say the things I was naturally too modest to point out myself.

"You see, there's a difference between being scared and acknowledging a potentially dangerous situation," Pookie continues. "Guido has raised a valid point here. We're potentially walking into a fight where the enemy has all the cards. It's worth thinking through before we commit ourselves."

"If the Boss says to do it, I'll do it," I sez with a shrug. "It won't be the first time I've walked into bad odds with my eyes open. But I still say if there's a good chance of us gettin' whacked, we should pass along what we've

found out so far first, so's the next crew doesn't have to
start from scratch."

Spyder kinda sags a bit like somebody let the air out
of her. All of a sudden, instead of lookin' like a junior
tough, she looks like a little kid that's been told she can't
go to the party.

"So we report back to the palace," she says in a flat
tone. "The wizard gets his information and there's no
more need for my services as a Royal Investigator. Sorry
if I was pushing it there for a while, Guido. It's just that
I've been having so much fun, I guess I wanted to try to
prolong it a little."

It becomes clear to me now what has been motivatin'
this big drive to continue the investigation. Spyder has
been havin' the time of her life hangin' out with Pookie
and me. Instead of bein' a misfit and fightin' every day
just to be accepted, we've been treatin' her like a favorite
kid sister. Particularly Pookie, who has been givin' her
tips on everything from how to dress sexy to how to take
out a couple of loudmouths without even mussin' her hair.

When this assignment is over, Pookie and I go back to
workin' with the rest of our usual crew, which as I have
said before are all top-notch both as fighters and as
friends. Spyder, on the other hand, would have to rejoin
her unit in the Army, an existence which, as I can testify
from first-hand experience, is drab at best. This is a fate
I would not wish on my worst enemy, much less someone
I have a fondness for as I do Spyder.

Pookie catches my eye with a look that sez that her
thoughts are runnin' along similar lines.

"Um, let's go over this all once more," I sez, stallin'
for time while I think. "Sure, I got my opinions, but I
don't like to think of myself as bein' closed-minded.
Maybe there's something I've been overlookin'."

Spyder starts to roll her eyes, then realizes that I might

be softening my position and tries to look attentive.

"There are two different groups that we know of," I sez.

"That's right," Pookie sez, pickin' up my cue. "The peek-a-boo crew in the Royal Game Preserve, and the clown in the costume."

I nod and start drumming my fingers thoughtfully.

"Now, of the two, the forest guys are the bigger potential threat. The question is, is there any way we can do a little more snoopin' around about them without actually goin' into the woods after them?"

"Didn't the sergeant say something about a subdivision close to the forest?" Pookie sez.

"Yeah. The Sherwood Arms," I sez. "So?"

"Well, what we seem to be confronted with is minor-league guerilla warfare," Pookie sez. "According to most military experts, guerrillas can't operate without popular, local support. Maybe we can pick up some information in that subdivision."

"I thought that they'd be living off the land," Spyder sez. "I mean, there must be plenty of game in the Game Preserve."

"Uh-huh," I sez. "Ever tried to actually eat wild game? It's not bad for an occasional variation from one's diet, but on a steady basis it's pretty bad, unless you have someone cookin' who really knows what they're doing."

"Besides," Pookie sez, "they've been swiping money from the tax collectors. You don't need gold if you're living off the land. It's a good bet that they're spending it somewhere. That subdivision seems like a logical choice."

"Sounds like a plan," I sez. "Shakin' down some locals for information is a lot more up my alley than tryin' to play Sneaky Pete through a bunch of bushes and swamps. What do you think, Spyder?"

"Whatever works for you guys," she sez, tryin' to sound casual.

Pookie gives me a big wink so's Spyder can't see. I decide that not hurryin' back to the palace isn't such a bad idea after all.

EIGHT

"You know, it's been so long since I've been away from Perv, I had forgotten what a hoot it can be visiting other dimensions," sez Pookie.

As I mentioned before, I had gotten into the habit of tuning out the ladies' conversations as we were travelin', as they tended to make my head hurt, but that comment caught my attention.

"What brings that to mind, Pookie?" I sez.

"Oh, just things you don't normally come across, like that . . . what did you call it again, Spyder?"

"A porta-pottie," sez Spyder?

"See? That's what I mean."

"What's so strange about that?" sez Spyder.

"Look around you, dear," sez Pookie. "We're surrounded by a wealth of bushes and trees. Why invent something like a porta-pottie?"

"You can't charge people for usin' a bush or a tree," I sez.

Pookie is silent for several minutes before she responds.

"You and your crew have been spending a lot of time at the Bazaar at D   l lately, haven't you, Guido?" she sez finally.

"That's right," I sez. "That's where our headquarters are. So?"

"Nothing," Pookie sez, innocent-like. "It just explains a couple things is all."

During our travels, I have learned that it's easier to get a straight answer out of a lawyer what knows you are both monied and guilty than it is to get Pookie to elaborate once she starts bein' evasive. As such I simply change the subject.

"Realizin' we are rapidly approachin' our destination," I sez, gesturing to the small clutter of buildings up ahead, "it might be a good idea if we got it straight as to what our modus operandi is goin' to be once we get there."

"Could you give me a quick briefing on the general layout here, Guido?" Pookie sez, eyein' the buildings. "What's the deal with these 'subdivisions', anyway?"

"It's a fairly recent development," I sez. "It used to be that people would move away from the small farmin' communities for the excitement and culture, not to mention the economic opportunities, of the bigger cities. The problem was, as more and more people came to the cities, it got crowded and tended to draw what is politely referred to as 'the rougher element' who make their livin's by separatin' said citizens from the gains from said economic opportunities.

"The solution, strange as it seems, is that those citizens who were successful enough to afford it retreated to areas midway between the cities and the farms. Developers bought up abandoned or strugglin' farms, slapped up clusters of houses, and sold them to people who work in the city, but don't want to live there. For the most part, the people we'll be talkin' to spend their days in the city workin', then travel here to the subdivisions evenings to sleep and spend time with their families.

"The older, better developed subdivisions, like the Sherwood Arms up ahead, have gotten large enough that they have their own cluster of small businesses providin' food, services, and sometimes limited entertainment, so their residents don't have to lug everything back from the city."

"So the folks in this subdivision think of themselves as ruthless, sophisticated city folk, but aren't actually tough enough to handle the mean streets, eh?" Pookie sez.

"That about sums it up," I sez.

"It that case," Pookie sez, "would you mind letting me take the lead on our first interrogation?"

"No problem," I sez. "You got a plan?"

"Nothing specific," she sez. "I just thought it might give me a chance to demonstrate to Spyder here the effectiveness of applied femininity. Do you understand what I'm saying, dear?"

"You're going to hit someone," Spyder sez, dutifully.

I barely manage to suppress a rude snicker. It is clear that civilizin' Spyder is not a task easily accomplished. Even for someone as polished and tenacious as Pookie.

"No, dear," Pookie sez, patiently. "Think carefully. Remember what we've been talking about in regards to subtlety?"

Spyder frowns with the unaccustomed effort of thinking. Then her expression brightens.

"You're going to threaten to hit someone," she sez, brightly.

This time my effort to suppress my reaction is less successful, and earns me a dirty look from Pookie.

"No, dear. That's Guido's department," she sez. "We're ladies. Tell you what. Just watch what I do and we'll talk about it later."

• • •

Unfortunately, my amusement with the situational did not last long. In fact, it dropped radically as soon as Pookie began her preparations.

Mostly, this consisted of using disguise spells to alter the appearances of both Spyder and myself. She said this was to make us look less intimidatin' so people would be more inclined to t   I think she was usin' the opportunity to exact a little revenge on us, as she maintained the same appearance she had when we was dealin' with the soldier types, and, if you'll recall, that was not exactly demure and unassumin'.

She let Spyder keep her new 'hot babe' look, but changed her outfit so it was no longer even a modified army uniform. Even so, the new civilian outfit was considerably less peek-a-boo provocative than it had been.

The real axe job she saved for me.

Now, I cannot argue with her basic logic, as there is no doubt that my normal appearance is both noticeable and awe-inspirin' and played no small part in my career choice. I mean, Mob enforcers tend to come in one of two body types: either the big and wide man-mountain model like Nunzio and myself; or the skinny, fast, and nasty knife-man model like Snake. Either style has the marked advantage of makin' regular folks want to co-operate with you without contestin' whether or not you are actually capable of uppin' the ante if they decide to be difficult. It was therefore understandable that she felt it necessary to lessen the impact of the visual impression I normally make on the uninitiated.

I do, however, think she went a bit overboard on said lessenin'.

First, she knocked about a third off me, both in height and in girth. Then she took my normally spiffy outfit and changed it to a drab overall kind of rig than hung on my "new body" like a coat draped over a small chair. The buck teeth were a totally unnecessary touch, as I did not plan on smilin' much while lookin' like this.

"That should just about do it," Pookie sez with a grin, steppin' back to survey me like an artist viewin' a still-damp canvas. "Just remember to keep your weapons out of sight unless we're actually attacked."

This last I figure was a bit of self-protection on her part, because the way I was feelin' after havin' viewed my new appearance, there was no doubt in my mind as to who my prime target would be if I should happen to decide to abandon my preferred peace-lovin' manner.

"Everybody ready?" she sez, finally. "Spyder? Guido?"

"It's your show," I sez with a shrug.

"All right. Just stay close and follow my lead."

We tags along as she ambles into the scattered groupin' of small businesses that seems to mark the hub of the subdivision. There is only a handful of people wanderin' about, and most of them seem to be of the housewife variety. In no time flat, however, she has singled out her first target. He is a lanky string-bean sort with fiery red hair. More notably to the practiced eye, his clothes are several notches more expensive than anyone else's who is immediately visible.

"Excuse me? Sir?" Pookie sez, hailin' him.

He glances around a couple times to be sure she is addressin' him, then comes over to where we are standin'.

"Yes, Miss? Can I be of assistance?" he sez.

Definitely an educated type.

"I certainly hope so," Pookie sez, givin' him her best smile. "Do you live around here?"

"As a matter of fact, I do," he sez, givin' the smile right back to her.

"Then maybe you can help us. You see, my associates and I have just arrived in your charming community and don't really know our way around. The thing is, we're supposed to be conducting a sort of a survey, and we don't have the foggiest of where to start."

"A survey? How fascinating."

As this exchange is goin' on the two of them are givin' each other the once over. Also the twice and three-times-over if you is actually countin'. Neither seems particularly disappointed with what they are seein'.

"Anyway, I was just saying to my assistants . . . Forgive me. My name is Pookie. And you are . . . ?"

"Will."

"Pleased to meet you, Will. You see, I was thinking that if we had the help of someone who really knew the area, we could get our job done in no time at all. That would free us up to explore whatever entertainment the local nightlife has to offer. Of course, you'd be welcome to join me . . . us . . . if you agree to help, that is."

She is layin' it on pretty thick, but the yokel is eatin' it up with a spoon and droolin' for more.

"It just so happens that I have the afternoon free . . . and the evening," he sez, his smile gettin' even wider. "What kind of a survey are you conducting?"

"We're just trying to find out what the local opinion is of the freedom fighters operating out of the Royal Game Preserve," Pookie sez.

All of a sudden, Will is not smilin'.

"Freedom fighters?" he sez.

"You know," Pookie sez with a wink, "the ones who have been running the tax vultures around in circles lately?"

The guy is now literally backin' away from her.

"I've never even heard of them," he sez. "No, ma'am. No knowledge at all. In fact, I don't think I'll be able to help you after all. Now, if you'll excuse me?"

"Maybe you can join us later?" Pookie sez, still tryin'.

"It occurs to me that probably wouldn't be such a good

idea," he sez. "People might get the wrong impression if we were seen together. You see, I'm married."

"I don't mind," Pookie sez. "Besides, marriage isn't anything a good lawyer can't fix."

"Lady, I *am* a lawyer," he sez. "And I've never fixed . . . I ever heard . . . Goodbye."

With that he turns on his heel and leaves, almost runnin' in his haste to put distance between him and us as we watch his retreat in bewildered silence.

"Well, that was instructive," Spyder sez.

"Ease up, Spyder," I sez before Pookie can go after her. "Tell me, Pookie, is it just me or was there something strange with the way that scene played?"

"Definitely something wrong there," Pookie sez, frownin'. "I could have sworn I had him hooked solid. Oh well, let me give it another try."

The next guy she runs her routine on is a big, athletic-lookin' individual named John we find loading one of those portapotties onto a wagon. Unfortunately, it's almost identical to what happened with Will, only without the polished language. John is all enthusiastic until she mentions the guys in the forest, then he practically tramples us makin' his getaway. As it turns out, John is also a married man.

"Either married men are a lot different in this dimension, or this is a very strange community," Pookie sez, her frustration startin' to show.

"I don't understand it either," I sez. "Tell you what, Pookie. Since they aren't respondin' to Beauty, what say we give the Beast a try?"

"Excuse me?" she sez, blinkin'.

I give her my best smile.

"Change me back to my normal appearance and let me give it a shot."

"Why not?" she sez. "I've been batting zero so far. In fact, while I'm at it, I'll give Spyder and myself a redo as well. That way we can always try the 'survey team' bit a try again later."

A few magical passes later, and I am my old self again. Mind you, a disguise spell doesn't actually change you physically, just your appearance. Still, it's good to know people are seein' the real me once again.

"Okay, Guido," Pookie sez, "it's your turn now. Pick your target."

"That place across the way looks as good as any," I sez, pointin'.

"Robb's Hardware and Sporting Goods?" Pookie sez, readin' the sign. "Okay. Anything we should do to back your play?"

"Nothin' special," I sez. "Just wander around the place slow and handle stuff. That and smile a lot."

With that, I lead the way across the street and through the doors into the store.

The guy behind the counter homes in on us as soon as we make our entrance, and not just because we're the only other ones in the place. As I noted earlier, my normal appearance tends to draw attention.

"Can . . . can I help you?" he sez, hesitantly.

Pookie and Spyder ignore him and start driftin' down the aisles, pickin' up stuff and lookin' at it careful before puttin' it down. I lean on the counter and do the talkin', lookin' around the place and not at the guy.

"I'd like to speak with the owner, if he has the time," I sez.

"I'm . . . That would be me," the guy sez. "I'm Robb."

"This is your establishment?" I sez, crankin' my head around to look at him direct for the first time.

"Well . . . Yes."

I go back to lookin' around, payin' particular attention to the ceiling.

"Nice little place you got here," I sez, thoughtful-like.

"Good location. Solid inventory. Yes sir. A really nice place. Shame if anything happened to it."

"Happened? Like what?" Robb sez, lickin' his lips.

"Ya never can tell," I sez. "A fire. Broken windows. Trouble with a small business is that it's a marginal operation. The littlest accident and it could go under, not to mention a lot of little accidents."

The guy is lookin' nervous now, and keeps glancin' at Spyder and Pookie. They're still handling things . . . real carefully . . . and smilin'.

"Um . . . Is there anything I can help you with?" he sez. "Anything specific you're looking for?"

"As a matter of fact," I sez, "what I'm lookin' for is some information. There's a rumor goin' around that I'm tryin' to run down."

"Well, there's a bar just down the street," Robb sez eagerly. "The bartender there knows everything about what's going on around here."

"You don't say? Right down the street, huh?" I brings my eyes back around to stare at him again. "The trouble with that is that I'm not down the street. I'm right here. And the one I'm talkin' to is you. You got a problem with that?"

"N . . . No. Of course not," he sez. "What is it that you wanted to know?"

"What it is, you see, is that I represent a . . . an association of businessmen," I sez. "They have heard that there is a group of individuals operatin' in this vicinity, specifically interfacin' with the kingdom's tax collectors when they is makin' their rounds. My employers are most anxious to speak with those individuals to ascertain if there is some way that they might work together to their mutual benefit. What I need is a means of contactin' those individuals to arrange such a meetin'."

"I . . . I really don't know what you're talking about," the guy sez.

"Do you want me to say it again?" I sez, raisin' my voice slightly. "Did I stutter?"

"No. I meant that I haven't heard anything about the group you're talking about," he sez. "Either group, actually. I just run my shop here and go home to the wife. Nobody ever tells me about anything."

"Well, think about it," I sez, givin' him a toothy smile. "Talk it over with the wife and see if you can't remember something. I'll probably be back to talk with you again. The thing is, if I find out that you know something and didn't share it with me, you might not see me comin' at all. Know what I mean?"

"I . . . I'll think about it," he sez. "But I really don't know anything."

I stare at him for a couple beats without sayin' anything, then turn and leave, gatherin' up Spyder and Pookie with my eyes as I go.

Nobody sez anything for a while as I lead the way out of the subdivision and away from the eyes of any onlookers. Finally, when we're well away, Spyder explodes.

"Wow, Guido! You were terrific! That was really great!"

"No it wasn't," I sez, slowin' down but still not lookin' at them direct.

"What do you mean?"

"Think about it, dear," Pookie sez. "It was a good show, but Guido didn't get any more information than I did."

"There's definitely something strange goin' on here," I sez, half to myself.

"I don't know. Maybe they really didn't know anything," Spyder sez.

"I don't buy it," I sez. "Even if they didn't have any specific information, they should have heard something, even if it was only rumors. That would be enough for them to try to impress Pookie, or to get me off their back when I leaned on them. No, there's some kind of coverup goin' on."

"That's the way it looks," Pookie nodded.

"You know, I've got an idea," Spyder sez. "It might be worth a try."

"What's that?" I sez.

"Well, these folks are money-motivated. Right? We could try posting a reward for information. If they won't respond to fear or lust, there's always greed."

Pookie and I looked at each other as we thought about it, then we both shook our heads.

"I don't think so, little sister," Pookie sez. "It's a nice thought, but when there's money on the table, it brings out all kind of false leads and wild goose chases. We'd go nuts trying to administer the thing, much less having to run down each and every rumor that got dropped on us."

"Besides," I sez, "if we're right and there's a coverup goin' on, anyone who talks to us is goin' to have the rest of the community down on them. Money is a great motivator, but it would take a lot of it to offset their fear of reprisals."

"Wait a minute, Guido," Pookie sez. "Maybe we're looking at this wrong. What if it isn't fear of reprisals that's keeping everyone quiet? What if it's money?"

"How's that again?"

"What if the gang is sharing their profits with the community?" she sez. "You know, robbing from the rich and giving to the poor? If the subdivision is getting a piece of the action, it's no wonder they won't talk about it to outsiders."

"I dunno," I sez. "It sounds pretty wild. I mean, I can understand the part about robbin' the rich. There's no money in robbin' the poor. But why would they be willin' to share it with anyone else? Besides, I didn't see any poor in that subdivision."

"I was speaking figuratively," Pookie sez. "But remember what I said about guerrillas needing popular support? Can you think of any better way for the gang to make themselves popular than by instituting a profit-sharing plan? Remember, they get to decide how much to share, and no one audits their books on the count. It could be a very shrewd and economical way to get and keep the people on your side against the authorities."

"I'll have to think about that one," I sez. "One thing for sure is we've hit a dead end on this line of inquiry. Maybe it's time to look up the clown with the costume."

What our team of investigators is not aware of is the repercussions of their visit to Sherwood Arms. Specifically, it created the need for an emergency meeting of the Sherwood Arms Bow Hunting Club that very evening.

"Com'on, Robb," Tuck was saying. "This whole thing was your idea. Now you have one person asking questions and you get spooked."

"I'm not spooked," Robb said. "I'm scared spitless. And if you saw the monster that was grilling me, you wouldn't call him 'one person'."

"If it's the same one that was with the vixen that was trying to get information out of me, he didn't seem like all that much," said Will.

"Definitely on the scrawny side," said John.

"Pipe down, you two," said Tuck, taking the lead for a change. "We've already decided there were two different groups asking questions, even if they both did have two women and one man."

"That's two too many if you ask me," Robb said. "Running the army around in circles in the woods is one thing, but this is getting too close to where we live. I say we should lay low for a while. Suspend operations until this sudden wave of interest dies down."

"Okay. No problem," Will said with a shrug. "Consider it done . . . or undone as the case might be."

"Just like that? No arguments?" Tuck said, cocking an eyebrow.

"Sure," said Will. "Think about it, Tuck. We've already hit the tax collectors once. How many times a year do you think they make those rounds, anyway?"

NINE

Our efforts to locate the lone raider was notably different from our previous venture in that this time around we was all equally unhappy . . . mostly with our appearance.

Again, it had been agreed upon that we should assume the least threatening disguises imaginable to encourage our mark to attack us, thereby negatin' the necessity of havin' to find him. To this end, Pookie had gone to work with her disguise spell.

When she was done, we was all not only wearin' army-type uniforms, we was all males. This was decided on in case word was out that there was a team of hunters out lookin' for outlaws consistin' of two females and a male. The problems began when Pookie insisted, just to be sure we drew an attack, that we should be kinda scrawny, puny-lookin' males. After havin' suffered through the embarrassment of such a disguise back at Sherwood Arms, Spyder and I took the position that if we had to look wimpy, then it was only fair that Pookie herself should also adopt a similar appearance. I feel that the duration and bitterness of the ensuin' argument before Pookie agreed only showed that, as competent a pro as she was, she was still vulnerable to a woman's vanity.

Our plan was as simple in its conception as it was borin' in its execution. Basically we was to re-trace the path of the tax collectin' team what had been ambushed by this joker, actin' like we was a different unit what got separated and was tryin' to re-group with the others. Logically, by revisitin' the same locales, this should draw the same attack as the army types had suffered, except we'd be ready for it. In actuality, this meant walkin' a long way and stoppin' in a lot of communities where army types are not really welcome, and doubly so since one tax team had already been through. The ladies was sure that the garbage, both verbal and literal, which was hurled at us as we passed through was on account of our less-than-heroic disguises. I, on the other hand, felt that it was aimed at army types in general regardless of the details of their appearance.

Of course, I kept this opinion mostly to myself. The only thing worse than arguin' with a woman when she's upset is arguin' with two women when they're upset . . . unless, perhaps, it's winnin' that selfsame argument.

"I still don't see why we have to keep wearing these stupid disguises when we're out of town and in the country," Spyder sez for maybe the twentieth time. "It's not like anyone can see us."

For some reason, this time her complaint draws an answer out of me . . . probably because I am already irritated myself. Maybe it's because it is the twentieth time she's made the same complaint. Then, too, maybe it is because I have been stuck pushin' the wheelbarrow that is part of our disguises as tax collectors. While said wheelbarrow speaks highly of the completeness of our disguises, the fact that I always seem to be the one pushin' it is a commentary on the lack of sexual equality within our group.

"We wear the disguises in town so that whoever is passin' the word to our target will see us as easy marks," I sez, flatlike. "The reason we wear them in the country is that when somebody does see us, specifically that same target, that we will look like the same easy marks what was spotted in town."

"Is something bothering you, Guido?" Pookie sez, cockin' her head at me. "You've been acting kind of tense and irritable lately."

"Maybe it's because, for all our disguises and round about walkin'," I sez, "I get the feelin' that we're not takin' this guy nearly seriously enough."

"Oh, c'mon, Guido," Spyder sez. "A clown running around in a costume complete with a mask and cape? Against the three of us? What's to worry about other than finding him in the first place?"

"Take it easy, little sister," Pookie sez. "Guido knows his business, and if he's worried I think we should listen. Okay, Guido . . . Talk to us. What are you seeing that we're missing in all this?"

"Aside from the basic premise that the most dangerous thing you can do is to underestimate your opponent," I sez, "there are the particulars in this situation. For example. Give me a description of the guy we're after."

The two of them look at each other, each waiting for the other to speak.

"Uh-huh," I sez. "He is, and I quote, 'a guy in a black costume with a mask and a cape.' End quote. Beyond that, we don't know anything about his height, build, or age, much less how much education shows in his speech patterns. He could have been sittin' at the next table when we stopped for lunch and we'd never know it."

"I see your point," Pookie sez, thoughtfully.

"It's an old trick," I sez with a shrug. "Wear something noticeable that people will remember when you work, and chances are that's all they'll remember. Take it off, and you fade into the crowd again."

"So you're saying that this guy might be smarter than we've been giving him credit for?" Pookie sez.

"Either that, or he's got someone advisin' him that know what he's doin'," I sez. "And that brings me to another particular. The one I'm watchin' for, the one that has me really worried, is the guy standin' back and coverin' him with a crossbow."

"How so?" sez Pookie.

"You might have missed it, but, accordin' to Sergeant Smiley, that individual is packin' a crossbow not unlike my own."

"That's important?"

"Pookie," I sez, "have you taken a look at my crossbow?"

"Not really," she sez. "I mean, I've seen it. But it's just a crossbow."

"I keep forgettin' that you spend most of your time on Perv or Deva or some of those other hi-tech dimensions," I sez.

"Yeah. So?"

"So allow me to advance your education in the area of the low-tech weaponry you seem to eschew."

With that, I remove my mini-crossbow from my belt, remove the quarrel, release the tension on the bow, and toss it to her gently.

She catches it one handed, then turns so that she'll have more light on it as she examines it. Her casual glance turns into a close stare, and her lips purse in a silent whistle.

"This is nice . . . very nice work," she sez.

"You don't know the half of it," I sez. "Try a snap shot. Don't aim, just instinct point."

She takes it in her right hand in a shooter's grip, spins, and levels it hip-high, focusin' on an imaginary target.

"Wow!" she sez in an awestruck voice. "That's balanced beautifully."

"Can I hold it?" Spyder sez.

After she gets the nod from me, Pookie passes it to her.

"That's a custom-made crossbow by Iolo," I sez. "It's the best I've seen in any dimension."

"Too bad he doesn't make one with a double bow that can give you two shots," Pookie sez, thoughtfully.

"He can do it," I sez, "but he doesn't like to. Talked me out of it when I asked."

"Really?"

"I don't know all the technicals," I sez with a shrug, "but it has something to do with a weakness in design when you go to a double bow. You don't get as accurate a delivery with either shot as you do with the single shot-model. I figure when you go to an expert, you should listen to what they have to say."

"Interesting," Pookie sez, retrievin' the weapon from Spyder and starin' at it anew.

"The point is that a bow like that costs roughly a year's wages for an average person in this dimension," I sez. "To own one, one either has to be very rich or very serious about one's weaponry. Since the guy in the opposition is currently in the highway-robbery business, I'm assumin' that he isn't rich. That makes him a serious armsman."

"Like you," Pookie sez, handing the beauty back to me.

"Uh-huh," I sez, reloadin' the weapon. "The fact is, I may even know him. The only ones I know who carry weapons from Iolo work for the Mob . . . or used to. Somehow I don't see this as their kind of action. Besides, Don Bruce, that's the guy who runs the Mob in these parts, has a deal goin' with the Boss to lay off the kingdom."

"Nonetheless," Pookie sez, "I see what you mean about taking these guys seriously."

"That's good," I sez, "since I've noticed some movement in that big tree up ahead. Don't look at it directly, but it's the one with the limb that juts out over the trail. I think we're finally gonna see some action."

TEN

Actually, it was a pretty feeble ambush. Particularly after the big buildup I had given it. Still, I hadn't managed to build and maintain the long career I am enjoyin' by underestimatin' the opposition . . . even when they deserve underestimatin'.

We are still a good ways from the tree, call it a stone's throw, when, with a snappin' of twigs and a small shower of leaves, this kid drops onto the trail ahead of us. He lands off balance and ends up on his rump, but he's game and manages to scramble back to his feet without droppin' his sword.

"Tell me again about how we were selling this guy short," Pookie murmurs to me.

I give a little shrug, as there is nothin' else to say.

I have to admit, the perpetrator does not strike an impressive figure. He's a short little runt, even with the hat, to a point where his head would maybe come halfway up my chest if I wasn't wearin' a disguise. He has the build of a gangly teenager and the grace of a three-legged mule, which he proceeds to demonstrate by gettin' his sword tangled in his cloak as he tries to brandish it. Despite the spiffy black outfit, I would figure that Spyder could take him and four more just like him without mussin' her hair.

"Good day to you, minions of Evil," he sez, tryin' to make his voice sound deeper. "I am here to relieve you of your troublesome burden. Your wheelbarrow is laden with monies taxed from the sweat of honest citizens. I will take charge of it from here."

Pookie and Spyder are lookin' at me with raised eyebrows, so I figure it's my show.

"I don't think so," I sez, foldin' my arms.

"Really?" the kid sez, genuinely surprised. "And why not, may I ask?"

"Well, other than the fact that we outnumber you three to one," I sez, "there the detail that we're all outside the range of that sword you're wavin'."

"Forgive me," he sez with a smile. "I neglected to introduce my associate. 'Nardo!"

"Perhaps you should count again, soldier," sez a voice to my right. "And believe me, you're well within my range."

I had marked that particular tree as bein' the most likely spot to give cover fire from, and I was right. The big guy had eased out from behind it just enough to get a clear shot if he had to, but could still duck back quick if things got rough. He had his crossbow loaded and cocked, all right, but at the moment he had it pointed straight up so we could get a good look at what he was holdin'.

"Well," I sez. "I guess there's only one thing I can say to that. Pookie! Drop the disguises!"

As I'm sayin' that last bit, I'm duckin' behind the wheelbarrow for cover as I pluck my own crossbow from my belt and level it at the kid.

Pookie and Spyder follow my earlier instructions and hit the dirt, movin' in opposite directions from where I am, then freeze. For several long moments, we hold that tableau without anyone sayin' anything.

"Is that you, Guido?" comes a call at last.

"Got it in one," I sez. "How's it goin', 'Nardo?"

"Not as good as it was a few seconds ago," he sez. "If I had spotted that you were a part of the guard detail, I would have passed on this caper."

"It's called a disguise spell," I sez. "It comes in handy when one is settin' up a counter-ambush. Wouldn't you agree?"

"I'll remember that next time . . . if there *is* a next time," he sez.

"So what are you doin' givin' cover fire on an amateur heist like this?" I sez. "I heard you retired."

"Took a baby-sitting job to make ends meet," he sez. "The baby is the one you're holding the crossbow on. How about yourself? What brings you to this neck of the woods?"

"At the moment I'm workin' an assignment as a Personal Envoy for the Great Skeeve," I sez. "It seems like you and your 'baby' there are a part of it."

'Nardo is silent for a while as he digests this.

"That's the way things are, huh?" he sez at last. "So where do we go from here?"

"I'd say it's time for us to talk," I sez. "You and me. Let's see if we can come up with a way for everybody to walk away from this one."

"Sounds good to me," he sez. "Let's do it."

He eases out from behind his tree while I stand up from behind the wheelbarrow. Then, movin' real slow and matching our pace to each other, we each ease sideways. He ends up standin' next to the kid, and I end up next to Spyder.

In hindsight, I probably should have gone with Pookie. At the time, however, Spyder was closer. Besides, I knew that Spyder could handle a crossbow because I had helped her learn back in Basic, while I wasn't sure whether or not Pookie's high-tech travels had familiarized her with this dimension's crossbow designs.

"Okay, Spyder," I sez, keepin' my eye on 'Nardo. "Take my crossbow and cover me. Keep it aimed at 'Nardo, but stay loose. We should be able to straighten this out without any shootin'."

"What's with all this talking, Guido?" she sez, takin' the crossbow from me. "You had the drop on them. Why not just finish it?"

"Take a tip from an old pro, Spyder," I sez. "If you have a choice between talkin' and fightin', always take the talk option. You can still fight if the talkin' doesn't work out. If you fight first, it's too late to talk."

I see that 'Nardo has handed his crossbow to the kid, so I start forward. As I do, I take care to move forward at an angle so I'm not in Spyder's line of fire and she has a clear shot at 'Nardo at all times. He does the same, movin' slow to meet me at a point where we is both in easy range of the coverin' crossbows.

It occurs to me that we each now have a crossbow pointed at us, held by kids what are not all that experienced. This is not a relaxin' thought, and I find myself wishin' that I had thought to mention to Spyder that the crossbow she is holdin' has a hair trigger on it, quite different from the army models she trained with.

"You're looking good, Guido," he sez as we come together.

"Thanks, 'Nardo. You're lookin' good yourself."

Actually, he looks kinda old to me. Even older than when I saw him before he retired. This does not seem like the moment to mention this, however.

"How's Nunzio?" he sez. "Are you two still working together?"

"He's fine," I sez. "He's back at the palace coverin' the Boss while I'm out here beatin' the bushes."

"Speaking of which, how do you propose we handle this situation?" he sez.

"First off, I've got one question," I sez. "Does the kid there have any intention of tryin' to whack the Great Skeeve or otherwise disrupt the current government of Posseltum?"

"Is that what this is all about?" he sez. "Naw. It's nothing like that. The kid overspent his allowance and is trying his hand at crime instead of getting a steady job. You know how that goes."

"I know the tune, I can fake the lyrics," I sez, makin' a face. "In that case, I think we can settle this pretty easily. You see, my specific assignment is to investigate rumored rebel activity, not to go chasin' highwaymen. If you give me your word that this is not part of a bigger caper, I think we can let the kid walk."

"You mean you'll let him go on hitting the tax collectors?" 'Nardo sez, surprised.

"I don't think that would be a good idea," I sez. "No, I meant that we won't take him in for what he's done so far. Throw a scare into him. Tell him that you got me to back off because we're old friends, but that if he keeps it up, I'll come after him for real. If you can't get him to go straight, at least convince him to pick targets that aren't tied into the government."

"What about the money from the first heist?" he sez.

"That's a good question," I sez. "Is there anything left from that?"

"Not much," 'Nardo sez. "Young as he is, the kid knows how to spend money."

"Tell you what," I sez. "I'll report that the attacks have been stopped. If the Boss wants to send me out to try to recover the loot, that will be a separate assignment. I don't think he'll bother, but even if he does, it will give you a big head start. Droppin' out of sight shouldn't be too tough. Just get him to dump that silly outfit."

"That's it then?" he sez. "We all just back away and everyone is happy?"

"It works for me," I sez with a shrug. "To be honest with you, the Boss . . . that's the Great Skeeve . . . isn't that much older than the kid there. We've gotten into some rough spots ourselves bailin' him out. It doesn't bother me at all that we all get off light on this one."

"I'm just glad we didn't have to go sideways to each other, Guido." 'Nardo sez. "However it came out, I wouldn't have liked the results."

"I guess that settles it," I sez. "Good luck to you, 'Nardo."

"And to you, my friend!"

Before I realize what he's doin', he steps forward and sweeps me into the big hug that's the traditional Mob greetin' and farewell.

There's a soft 'twang' behind me and I barely have time to shove him away when something slams into my arm.

"I didn't mean to do it, Guido. Honest!"

This is maybe the twelfth time Spyder has made this statement.

"It's okay, Spyder. Really," I sez. "These things happen. It goes with the job."

This is the same response I have given each time she has made her declaration. In fact, it is the same, word for, word. I have a little trouble comin' up with original lines or variations when I've been shot. Still, Spyder is still upset, so I do my best to calm her down.

"I mean, I didn't really mean to shoot," she sez . . . again. "He surprised me when he stepped forward like that, and when I shifted to keep him covered, the cross-bow just went off."

"It's my fault, really," I sez, tryin' to make light of it.

"I should have warned you about the hair-trigger. Cheer up. It could have been a lot worse."

"You're right! I could have killed you! Oh, Guido. I'm so sorry."

As you can tell, my efforts to calm her down have been less than sucessful.

"He knows you're sorry, dear," Pookie sez, takin' a hand. She has been bandagin' my arm and is now riggin' a sling. "Why don't you take a little walk and compose yourself while Guido and I finish up here?"

"Okay," Spyder sez, hangin' her head. She starts to go, then stops with her back to me. "Guido? I really am sorry."

She strides off before I can say anything in return.

"So, what do you think we should do now?" Pookie sez, finishin' the sling.

"I'm thinkin' we head back to the palace," I sez. "We've taken the investigation about as far as we can, so it's time to check in with the others and get their opinions on what to do next, if anything. Besides, with this ding in my arm I could use a little downtime before I go huntin' for any more trouble."

"If you don't mind, I think I'll stay out a while," Pookie sez. "Maybe keep Spyder with me. She could use a little more seasoning."

"Fine by me," I sez. "If you want, I'll send along some help. Maybe Nunzio."

"That would be great," she sez. "I think we'll be hanging around the Sherwood Arms subdivision. See if we can find out anything more about that crew that's working the game preserve. And Guido?"

"What?"

"When you get back to the palace, could you do me a favor? Could you say that I was the one who shot you accidentally, not Spyder?"

I give her a long look.

"Why would you want me to say that?"

"Like you said, it was an accident. It could have happened to anyone who wasn't familiar with the hair-trigger rig you use . . . Spyder or me."

"Uh huh," I sez. "So why do you want to make it you instead of Spyder?"

"You know this is only a temporary job for me," she sez. "I mean, I enjoy working with this crew, but I figure I'll be moving along eventually. I think Spyder would like to try to join your crew on a permanent basis once she gets out of the army. Of the two of us, I think it would be better if the accident went on my record instead of hers."

"If that's the way you want it," I sez.

Secretly, though, I have my doubts about Spyder as a permanent member of our crew. While I'm not one to hold a grudge, I've found in the past I have trouble relaxing around someone who's shot me. Even if it was by accident.

ELEVEN

It was late when I got back to the palace. I probably could have stretched the trip out a bit, but instead I pushed it straight through.

Investigatin' the trouble with the tax collectors had been a welcome break from the palace routine, but that was done now . . . at least, temporarily. Now I found my mind turnin' once more to the problems at the palace. The more I thought about it, the quicker I walked.

The Boss was in a spot. He either had to marry Queen Hemlock and help her run the kingdom, or turn her down, in which case she threatened to abdicate and stick him with runnin' it by himself. The trouble was that the problem involved dealin' with a woman, which was the Boss's weak suit. The Great Skeeve might be quick on his feet and faster with his brain when it came to magik, but plain old Skeeve was a babe in the woods where women were concerned. What was more, there wasn't much I could do as a bodyguard to help him . . . except maybe seein' to it that Queen Hemlock didn't try to whack him if she didn't like his answer.

I was still thinkin' about all this when I finally reached the palace. Luckily, it was late enough that I figured everyone would have gone to bed, so I wouldn't have to worry about reportin' in until tomorrow. That would give me time to sort out what I was gonna say, and ensure that I had a clear head when it came to dealin' with questions. With that in mind, I headed for my room.

"Back already, Guido?" comes a voice from the shadows. "How did it go?"

I turn toward the voice as Aahz emerges from the shadows.

Now, I have to admit that Aahz is not my favorite member of the team. By this I do not mean he is not capable, as even without his powers he is able to hold his own in a brawl against all comers and is as shrewd and knowledgeable as anyone I have ever met. What keeps me from warmin' to him is his social skills, or lack thereof. He started out as the Boss's mentor, and even though that relationship was upgraded to a full partnership, he still tends to lean on Skeeve publicly more than I think is necessary. In fact, his idea of relatin' to most people ranges from impatient sarcasm to open scorn. While I figured that I'd have to report to him sooner or later, my own preference was leanin' toward later.

"Oh. Hi, Aahz," I sez. "What are you doin' up so late?"

"I was just sitting and thinking," he sez. "Enjoying the night air. Come on over and join me and fill me in on what happened."

Not really havin' much choice, I follow him back into the shadows. There is a wide opening in the wall of the corridor that looks out over the palace's courtyard . . . the keep, I think they call it. Aahz sits on the low wall that is there to keep people from fallin' out, and gestures for me to take a seat next to him.

"So, what's the word?" he sez. "Did you find any signs of a brewing rebellion?"

"Not really," I sez. "We checked in with the tax boys, and they've been havin' a bit of trouble with havin' their collectors ambushed. Two different groups, it seems. It sounds to me, though, that it's more like a couple groups tryin' for some easy money than an actual rebellion."

My eyes are adjustin' to the dark, and I can see Aahz noddin' slowly.

"Tell me more," he sez.

"Well, there are a bunch of guys workin' out of the Royal Game Preserve," I sez. "They're usin' bows and makin' hit-and-run guerrilla attacks from the woods and underbrush. I figured that with only the three of us, it wouldn't be real smart to try to go into the woods after them."

"Good thinking."

"We did do some askin' around tryin' to get a line on them," I continued, "but everyone clammed up as soon as we raised the subject. We have a theory that the locals are hidin' them, maybe for a share of the loot."

"Interesting," Aahz sez. "And the other group?"

"That was just a couple of stick-up artists," I sez.

"Was?"

"Well, we sort of rigged an ambush and drew them out into the open," I sez. "I don't think they'll be botherin' us again."

"Is that where you picked up the arm wound?" Aahz sez. I see his teeth flash in the darkness as he smiles. "How many bodies did you leave behind?"

Well, I knew I was gonna have to deal with this eventually.

"None," I sez. "Actually, all we did was throw a major scare into them. The arm was an accident while Pookie was coverin' me."

"Pookie shot you?"

"Like I say, it was an accident," I sez with a shrug. "I passed her my custom crossbow, but forgot to warn her about the hair trigger. If it's anybody's fault, it's mine."

There is a long moment of silence, and I think Aahz is buildin' up to one of his explosions. Then I hear him sigh.

"She always was a little quick on the trigger," he sez. "Sorry, Guido. I should have warned you about that before I let her tag along."

It occurs to me that this is the first time I've heard Aahz apologize to me . . . or anyone else, for that matter.

"That's okay," I sez, a little off balance. "No real harm done."

"When you get a chance, check in with Massha," he sez. "She should have something in her magik gimmick collection that will speed up the healing on that arm."

"Uh . . . Thanks, Aahz," I sez, still a little confused by his new, mellow attitude.

"Other than that, it sounds like you did a good job, Guido. All of you," he sez. "It'll be good to have you all back."

"Actually," I sez, "Pookie and Spyder are still out. They're doin' a bit more checkin' on that forest group. I just came in because of the arm. I was gonna talk to the Boss about sendin' Nunzio out to replace me as their backup man."

"Sounds like a plan," Aahz sez. "Again, nice work. I don't think I've ever said it, Guido, but I've always admired your professionalism. Nunzio's, too. For short-lived humans who have never studied magik, you're both remarkably effective."

An apology and a compliment in one conversation. I am now definitely confused, so I counter by changin' the subject.

"Thanks, Aahz," I sez. "So what's been goin' on around here? Is the Boss okay?"

There is another long silence. So long, in fact, that I

am startin' to get scared about what the news is gonna be.

"I'm afraid Skeeve may be in over his head this time," Aahz sez at last. "You were right about keeping this rebellion thing from him. He's confused and desperate enough without fretting about how the *hoi polloi* are reacting to the situation."

I suddenly realize what is goin' on.

Aahz is worried about the Boss. Worried big time.

I always knew that Aahz was fond of his partner, but usually he showed it with bluster and lectures. Seein' him like this, quietly concerned, makes me realize how deep his feelin's really ran. It changes my opinion of him . . . for the better.

"It's a tough one, all right," I sez. "Different than any of the other capers we've been in on. Still, I figure the Boss has us to help him, so he'll probably pull through."

"By 'us' I assume you mean you and Nunzio," Aahz sez.

"Actually," I sez, "I was talkin' about the whole M.Y.T.H. Inc. crew, not the least of which includes you. That's one of the main reasons I got involved with the Mob in the first place, you know. You can only do so much alone. As part of a group, you got teammates to cover your back. Sometimes their strengths can make up for your weaknesses."

"I never really thought of it that way," Aahz sez, "but you've got a point."

He's quiet for a while, then opens up again.

"You know, I almost didn't come back from Perv," he sez. "I was settling in and getting ready to work solo again."

I didn't know that, but, as I said, Aahz and I didn't really talk all that much . . . and not at all since he and the Boss came back from Perv.

"What changed your mind?" I sez.

"The fact that Skeeve came all the way to Perv looking for me, particularly when the team had just been saddled with a rough assignment, was flattering," he sez. "I thought I'd tag along for one more round to see if I could help."

I could see him shake his head in the darkness.

"So I come back, and look what we're into," he sez. "I'll tell you, Guido, there are some situations that simply can't be handled with magik or muscle, or even a combination of both."

"Like I said, that's why we have teammates," I sez. "Friends can help turn a situation around . . . and even if they can't, you're not facin' the consequences alone."

Aahz heaved a big sigh.

"I guess that's the answer," he sez. "Thanks for listening, Guido. I'll see you tomorrow."

That is my cue to resume the trek to my room. The conversation with Aahz has given me a lot of food for thought, though.

I'm almost at my door when I hear voices. Angry voices arguin' loud.

The sound is comin' from the Boss's room.

TWELVE

I listen for a minute at the door, then knock loudly.

The Boss answers, half lookin' back over his shoulder at the man and woman shouting at each other behind him.

"Is everything okay, Boss?" I sez. "I thought I heard voices."

"Sure," he sez. "It's just . . . Guido? What are you doing back? And what happened to your arm?"

I am payin' more attention to the battlin' duo, who do not seem to have noticed my appearance yet. Neither of them is anyone I know as an associate of Skeeve's. If anything, they look a little foreign . . . though that might be because of their funny outfits.

"What's goin' on in there, Boss? Who are those two jokers, anyway?"

I am not likin' the look of this at all. While Nunzio and me take our bodyguardin' duties seriously, we usually figure the Boss is safe in his own room.

"Oh, those are just a couple friends of mine," he sez. "Well . . . sort of friends. I thought they were just drop-

ping by to say 'Hi,' but, as you can see, things seem to
have gotten a little out of hand. The one with the beard
is Kalvin, and the lady he's arguing with is his wife,
Daphnie."

"Did you say 'his wife'?"

"That's right," he sez. "Why?"

That settles it.

"Get out of here, Boss." I sez, beckonin' him through
the door.

"What?"

As I have noted before, the Boss is often not real quick
on the uptake. "Boss, I'm your bodyguard. Right? Well,
as your bodyguard and the one currently responsible for
the well bein' of your continued health, I'm tellin' you to
get out of here!"

"But . . ."

I try to be patient, but enough is enough. Without botherin' to argue further, I scoop him up with my good arm
and carry him out into the corridor before settin' him
down again.

"Now stay here," I sez. "Got that? Stay here!"

I feel a little like Nunzio talkin' to Gleep, but the message seems to finally get through.

"Okay, Guido," he sez. "Here it is."

I give him the hairy eyeball for a moment to be sure
he means to stay put, then turn and re-enter the room,
shutting the door behind me.

The two continue to ignore me as I decide how to pro-
ceed. It is not all that easy to think, as they is makin'
enough noise to drown out a busy kitchen durin' the lunch
rush.

Finally, I recall watchin' Nunzio one time, back when
he was teachin', and decide to give one of his techniques
a try. Without movin' any closer or gettin' between them,
I start to clap my hands together as loud as I can. This
distracts them, and they turn their attention on me.

"Who are you and what do you think you're doing?" the guy with the beard sez.

"What I am is standin' between you and the B . . . Skeeve," I sez. "What I'm doin' is shuttin' down this party."

"This is a private discussion," the doll sez. "You have no right interfering."

"Yes, ma'am. You're right," I sez, politely. "It's a private discussion between the two of you and I think it should be continued in private . . . not in someone else's home. Know what I mean?"

"Oh, come on, dear," the guy sez. "Let's get out of here."

I think he is gonna head out the door, but instead there's a BAMPF and he disappears into thin air. She favors me with one last glare, then vanishes with a BAMPF of her own.

Demons.

I wait a few moments to be sure they're gone, then open the door again.

"You can come in now, Boss."

"All right, Guido," he sez. "What was that all about?"

Now that the crisis is past, I figure it is wise to revert to my normal polite manner.

"Sorry to barge in like that, Boss," I sez. "You know that's not my normal style."

"So what were you doing?"

"What I was doin' was my job," I sez, patiently, still a little worked up from the situation. "As your bodyguard, I was attemptin' to protect you from bein' hurt or maybe even killed. It's what you pay me for, accordin' to my job description."

"Protecting me? From those two?" he gives me a smirk. "C'mon, Guido. They were just arguing. They weren't even arguing with me. It was a family squabble between the two of them."

"Just arguing? What do you think . . ."

I pause and take a long, slow breath, tryin' desperately
to get my nerves under control.

"Sorry, Boss. I'm still a little worked up over that close
call. I'll be all right in a second."

"What close call? They were just . . ."

"I know, I know. They were just arguin'."

I take a deep breath and flex my arms and hands, tryin'
to relax.

"You know, Boss, I keep forgettin' how inexperienced
you are. I mean, you may be tops in the magik department, but when it comes to my speciality, which is to say
rough-and-tumble stuff, you're still a babe in the wood-
work."

I figure this is as good a time as any to further the
Boss's education, so I elaborate.

"You see, Boss, people say that guys like Nunzio and
me are not really all that different from the cops . . . that
it's the same game on different sides of the line. I dunno.
It may be true. What I am sure of, though, is that both
we and our counterparts agree on one thing: The most
dangerous situation to stick your head into . . . the situation most likely to get you dead fast . . . isn't a shoot-out
or a gang war. It's an ordinary D & D situation."

"D & D?" he sez with a frown. "You mean that game
you were telling me about with the maps and dice?"

"No," I sez, patient-like. "I'm talkin' about a 'domestic
disturbance.' A family squabble . . . just like you had
goin' on here when I came in. They're deadly, Boss. Especially one between a husband and wife."

"Are you kidding, Guido?" the Boss sez. "What could
happen that would be dangerous?"

"More things than you can imagine," I sez, grim like.
"That's what makes them so dangerous. In regular hassles,
you can pretty much track what's goin' on and what might
happen next. Arguments between a husband and wife are
unpredictable, though. You can't tell who's gonna swing

at who or with what, because they don't know themselves."

"Why do you think that is, Guido? What makes fights between married couples so explosive?"

"I never really gave it much thought," I sez. "If I had to give an opinion, I'd say it was due to the motivationals."

"The motives?"

"That, too." I frown, wonderin' why he is repeatin' what I said. "You see, Boss, the business-type disputes which result in violence like I am normally called upon to deal with have origins that are easily comprehended . . . like greed or fear. That is to say, either Boss A wants somethin' that Boss B is reluctant to part with, as in a good-sized hunk of revenue-generatin' property, or Boss B is afraid that Boss A is gonna try to whack him and decides to beat him to the punch. In these situationals, there is a clear-cut objective in mind, and the action is therefore relatively easy to predict and counter. Know what I mean?"

"I think so," he sez. "And a domestic disturbance?"

"That's where it can get ugly," I sez with a grimace. "It starts out with people arguin' when they don't know why they're arguin'. What's at stake there is emotions and hurt feelin's, not money. The problem with that is that there is no clear-cut objective, and as a result, there is no way of tellin' when the fightin' should cease. It just keep escalatin' up and up, with both sides dishin' out and takin' more and more damage, until each of them is hurt so bad that the only important thing left is to hurt the other one back."

I pause and shake my head.

"When it explodes, you don't want to be anywhere near ground zero. One will go at the other or they'll go at each other, with anything that's at hand. The worst part is, and the reason neither us or the cops want to mess with it, is that if you try to break it up, chances are they'll both turn on you. You see, mad as the are, they'll still reflexively protect each other from any outside force . . . into which category will fall you or anyone else who tries to interfere. That's why the best policy, if you have a choice at all, is to get away from them and wait until the dust settles before venturin' close again."

"I think I understand now, Guido," he sez. "Thanks. Now tell me, what happened to your arm? And what are you doing back at the palace?"

The sudden change of subject catches me off balance.

"Sorry I didn't check in as soon as I got back," I sez, stallin' for time. "It was late and I thought you were already asleep . . . until I heard that argument in process, that is. I would have let you know first thing in the morning."

"Uh-huh. No problem. But since we're talking now, what happened?"

"We ran into a little trouble, is all," I sez, casual-like. "Nothin' serious."

"Serious enough to put your arm in a sling," he sez. "So what happened?"

"If it's okay with you, Boss, I'd rather not go into details. Truth is, it's more than a little embarrassin'."

"All right," he sez. "We'll let it ride for now. Will you be able to work with that arm?"

"In a pinch, maybe. But not at peak efficiency. That's really what I wanted to talk to you about, Boss. Is there any chance you can assign Nunzio to be Pookie's backup while I take over his duties here?"

"I don't know, Guido. Nunzio's been working with Gleep to try to figure out what's wrong with him. I kind of hate to pull him off that until we get some answers. Tell you what. How about if I talk to Chumley about helping out?"

"Chumley?" I sez. "I dunno, boss. Don't you think that

him bein' a troll would tend to scare people in these parts?"

"Doesn't Pookie have a disguise spell or something that would soften Chumley's appearance?" he sez. "I was assuming that she wasn't wandering around the countryside showing the green scales of a Pervect."

"Hey! That's right! Good idea, Boss. In that case, no problem. Chumley's as stand-up as they come."

"Okay. I'll talk with him in the morning."

"Actually, Chumley's a better choice than Nunzio," I sez, warmin' up to the idea. "Pookie's still kinda upset abut shootin' me, and Nunzio would probably . . ."

"Whoa! Wait a minute. Did you say Pookie shot you?"

Now I am annoyed with myself. After havin' successfully dodged the question earlier, I have proceeded to re-introduce the subject all by myself.

I decide to settle this once and for all by takin' it on head on . . . with a bluff.

"Really, boss," I sez, hurt-like, drawin' myself up to my full height. "I thought we agreed that we wasn't gonna talk about this. Not for a while, anyway."

With that I make my exit, with as much dignity as I can muster.

THIRTEEN

"No trouble at all, old boy. Glad to help. Could use a change of scenery, really."

This is Chumley talkin'. I came to see him as soon as I rolled out in the morning to ask him about bein' backup muscle for Pookie and Spyder. As a Troll, he is probably the strongest, toughest member of our team, next to Nunzio and me, even if he does talk funny when he isn't workin'.

"The Boss was sayin' that Pookie could take care of your appearance with her disguise spell," I sez.

"Actually, that won't be a problem," he sez. "Little sister left me a gizmo that should handle things. Where did I put that?"

He rummages around in a drawer and comes up with a device I recognize. I had seen his sister, Tananda, use it when we worked together briefly on our last assignment.

It looks like one of those mirror-compact rigs that the dolls use, except this one has a couple dials that, if you knew how to manipulate them, could change your ap-

pearance just like a disguise spell. That much I know.
How to use the thing I haven't a clue.

"So, you're all set?" I sez. "When do you figure you
can get started?"

"Oh, there are a couple things I've got to finish up first,
then I'll be ready," he sez. "It would also probably be
discreet to wait until I heard officially from Skeeve before
embarking. Don't you think?"

This takes me a bit aback.

He's right, of course. Usually team assignments are
handed out by the Boss. The trouble is that havin' rigged
things to investigate the so-called rebellion without
clearin' it with the Boss, plus pretty much captainin' the
team while we were in the field, has gotten me in the
habit of independent action. Of course, as I mentioned
earlier, in the Mob such habits of independence are not
necessarily conducive to one's continued health.

"Of course," I sez, not lettin' on that I overlooked that
loop. "I guess I'm just kinda anxious to get things rollin'
so's Pookie won't have to operate too long alone."

"From what I've seen of Pookie," Chumley sez, "she
seems quite capable of taking care of herself . . . and several others, besides."

I am glad Chumley has not asked for details about my
wounded arm. Even though she asked me to do it, I am
not really comfortable attributin' Spyder's error to Pookie.

"Well, I'm off to see Massha," I sez.

"Tell her 'Hi' for me," he sez. "I may not get a chance
to stop and see her before I go. Besides, frankly, I find
all her preparations for the wedding to be a little unnerv-
ing."

"You know," I sez, shakin' my head, "I still can't believe that neither the Boss nor Aahz said anything to me
about Massha gettin' married. I saw both of 'em when I
got in last night, and neither of them even mentioned it."

"They both seem to have a lot on their minds these

days," Chumley sez. "Besides, Massha seems to be taking care of the arrangements herself, so they haven't really been that involved . . . so far."

As I make my way to Massha's room, however, it occurs to me that this is yet another example of how the way the Boss does things differs so radical-like from other Mob operations. In the regular Mob, a marriage is a major event. Comin' in second only to the attention they give funerals.

"You just sit right there, Guido, honey. Massha has just the thing to fix up that arm of yours . . . if I can just lay my hands on it."

"Will it hurt?" I sez, a little nervous. I have never tried magical healin' before, and am uncertain as to what it involves.

"A little more than amputation, but you'll still have your arm," she sez, distracted.

"Are you kiddin' me?" I sez, lookin' toward the door.

"Of course I'm kidding you," she sez, laughin'. "Don't be such a baby. Honestly. Men. Always so ready to get into a fight, and such little boys when it comes to healing up afterward. Really, you won't feel a thing. Ah! Here we are!"

She comes up with a tube of something from which she then proceeds to squeeze a glob of creamy goo over my wound. It glows and sparkles for a moment, then seems to soak right into the skin, leavin' no trace behind. I'll have to admit, she is correct. Not only does it not hurt, it feels sort of cool and soothing.

"There we are," she sez. "The muscle will probably be a bit sore for a while, so you might want to leave the sling on. It should be good as new by tomorrow."

"Thanks, Massha," I sez, flexing my arm cautiously.

Frankly, I am amazed. Not by the healin', though I'll admit it was pretty impressive, but by the fact she could find it at all.

Chumley told me that Massha has changed quarters, but he always did have a gift for understatement. Her new room is roughly the size of a small warehouse, makin' it roughly three times the size of either of the rooms Nunzio and I have. Even with the extra acreage, however, it is crammed to the walls.

There are bolts of cloth and drawin's piled everywhere. Shoes and fabric samples and jewelry are scattered about in seemingly careless abandon, and there is not one but four full-sized sewin' dummies lined up in the center of the room. Realizin' that Massha is of the extra-extra-extra-extra-enormous size, this gives the feelin' that I am suddenly facin' the front line of a heavy contact-sport team after I have shrunk considerably.

The fact that she could find a small tube of goo in the middle of this chaos is nothin' short of miraculous.

I also find myself revisin' my earlier thoughts about this wedding not bein' a big deal. Judgin' from what Massha has goin', this event promises to make the biggest shindig the Mob has thrown look like a Tupperware party.

"By the way, Massha," I sez, "I guess congratulations or best wishes or whatever are in order. The General is a lucky man."

I mean this sincerely. After gettin' over the initial shock and thinkin' it over carefully, I have concluded that Massha is a real catch . . . ignorin' the possible parallels to big-game trophies. While it is true that she is large to the point of bein' intimidatin', especially takin' into account her taste in clothes and jewelry which run to extreme of loud and flashy, the fact remains that the biggest thing about her is her heart. Underneath her brash and pushy exterior, Massha is perhaps the kindest, gentlest soul it has ever been my privilege to meet. General Badaxe could do a lot worse in pickin' a life partner.

"Thanks, Guido," she sez, startin' to tear up a little. "I still have trouble believing that it's really happening. I never thought . . . I mean, with the way I look . . ."

She breaks off and blows her nose loudly, a sight which I will spare you the description of, bein' both a merciful and weak-stomached individual.

"So, how are the wedding plans coming?" I sez, tryin' to lighten the mood. "How are the pompous and circum-stantials goin'?"

"It's utter madness," she sez, regainin' her composure. "Still, things are staggering along. The Queen has been a big help."

"The Queen? You mean Queen Hemlock?"

Things are suddenly adding up a bit. Massha is not only one of the M.Y.T.H. Inc. crew, she is also the Boss's apprentice . . . and Queen Hemlock has designs on the Boss. Of course she'll spare no expense in helpin' set up this wedding.

"That's right. She really has been a dear. To be honest, I think she's hoping our little ceremony will be a dress rehearsal for her own wedding."

"That was occurrin' to me as well," I sez. "What are your thoughts on that, Massha?"

"Frankly, I have some serious doubts about the whole thing," she sez. "I mean, marriage seems so right for Hugh and me. It's something we both really want, so it's going to happen whatever we have to wade through to get there. It seems to me that the only reason Skeeve is considering marrying Queen Hemlock is that he feels he has to. To me, that's a lousy basis for a marriage."

Some women get a little crazy on the subject of mar-riage, especially when they're in the process themselves, thinkin' how it's the best thing in the world for everyone. I am glad to hear that Massha is not of the ilk.

"Sounds like good thinkin' to me," I sez. "Oh well. I better be movin' along now. You've got lots to do, and I still haven't checked in with Nunzio yet. Thanks again for the healin'!"

While it has been good to get back and see the various members of our team, I will admit it is a particular relief when I finally get a chance to sit down alone with Nunzio. What with him bein' my cousin, we have known each other since before Don Bruce assigned us to the Boss, and before that, even before we joined the Mob in the first place. If there is anyone I can speak my mind to without first havin' to think things through, it's Nunzio. What's more, because we know each other so well, we also know when to ask each other embarrassin' questions and when to maintain a tactful silence.

Case in point: when I first come into his room, he cocks an eyebrow at my arm in a sling and sez "Rough opposition?" to which I reply "Nothin' we couldn't handle." Beyond that, he has not pressed for details. That's the way it is with us. One of us will express curiosity, and if the other does not volunteer particulars, we simply let it drop.

I have given him a sketchy account of our mission, and he has supplied a brief update on the news and gossip in the palace.

"So, how's the Boss holdin' up through all this?" I sez.

Instead of answerin', Nunzio rubs his chin like he always does when he's thinkin' hard, then shakes his head.

"I dunno, Guido," he sez. "To be honest with you, he's been kinda weird."

Now, I know that the Boss has been under a lot of pressure what with tryin' to get the kingdom's finances squared away and havin' the Queen proposin' marriage to him, but we've seen him under pressure before. 'Weird' is not usually a word that Nunzio uses to describe the actions of a superior in the chain of command.

"Could you give me a 'for example' on that, cuz?" I sez.

"Well, you know how I've been workin' with Gleep, the Boss's dragon, to try to figure out why he's been attacking people?"

"Yeah?"

"Well, the Boss has it in his head that Gleep is intelligent."

"So what?" I sez. "The Boss has always had a soft spot for the little dragon. He's said all along that Gleep is a lot smarter than anyone gives him credit for."

"Not smart," Nunzio sez. "Intelligent. It's not that he's smart about learning tricks or recognizing people. The Boss thinks that Gleep may actually be intelligent, as in planning and scheming. He thinks that Gleep may be attacking people on purpose and trying to make it look like accidents."

I have to admit that is a crazy thought, though even considerin' it as a possibility is scary. But Nunzio isn't finished.

"And another thing," he sez, "the other day, the Boss asked me my opinion. Not on rough-and-tumble stuff, mind you. He wanted to know what I thought about his personal habits."

"He did what?" I sez, blinkin' with surprise.

Now, this is truly unheard of. When one is workin' as a Mob bodyguard, one observes and adapts to the habits of the body one is guardin' in order to be effective. Commentin' on those habits is not only unnecessary, it is ill-advised. Bein' asked to comment on those habits, particularly by the body itself, is inconceivable. It would be like askin' your armor if it thought you had smelly armpits.

"What? You think I'd make something like this up?" Nunzio sez, a little hurt. "I'm telling you the Boss made a point of asking me if I thought he drank too much. What's more, when I tried to hem and haw my way out of answering, he kept pushing and insisting that I give him an honest answer."

"Well, is he? Drinkin' too much, I mean," I sez.

"I really never thought about it," Nunzio sez. "I mean, sure he drinks. And he's been drinking more since he and Aahz got back from Perv. But how much is too much? Know what I mean? And why should he ask me?"

"Yeah," I sez. "Weird."

We are both ponderin' this in silence when there is a knock on the door and Aahz pokes his head into the room.

"Good," he sez. "I caught you both here. It's payday, boys. Thought I'd bring yours up since I was headed this way."

With that, he tosses us each a small sack of gold. I say 'small' in that it isn't one of the big bags like the tax collectors use. More like the size of my fist. Realizin', however, the size of my fist, the amount of gold bein' given us is far from paltry.

I glance over at Nunzio, and see that he is as surprised as I am.

"Ummm . . . Did we get a raise or something that I missed hearin' about?" I sez, heftin' the sack in my hand.

"Extra pay for the whole crew for helping out the kingdom," Aahz sez with a wink. "Bunny negotiated it."

"Nice," Nunzio sez, his eyebrows still up.

"Yeah. Well, thanks Aahz," I sez.

"No trouble," he sez. "By the way, I wouldn't want to try to tell you your business as bodyguards, but you might want to wander down to Grimble's."

"What's up?"

"I just sent Skeeve down there to pick up his pay, and believe me, it's more than ours put together. That's an awful lot of gold for him to be carrying around unescorted."

FOURTEEN

We are waitin' when the Boss emerges from Grimble's office. As Aahz predicted, the sack he is carryin' is substantially larger than the ones given to Nunzio and me, to a point where he is usin' two hands to carry it.

He strides on past us without so much as a 'Hello,' which, to say the least, is quite unlike him.

Nunzio and I exchange glances, then fall in behind him. Truth to tell, I do not think he is even aware we are there. He just marches along kind of mutterin' to himself without lookin' either left or right. Naturally, the procession we are makin' draws a certain amount of attention, but the people who notice us take one look at the Boss's expression and leave us alone.

The silence lasts until we reach the door of the Boss's room. Then, as he's openin' the door, he seems to notice us for the first time, raisin' his eyebrows like we had just interrupted him in the middle of something.

"You gonna want us for anything, Boss?" I sez, just to

start the conversation. "You want we should wait around out here?"

"Whatever, Guido," he sez with a wave, not even lookin' at us. "I'm going to be here for a while, though, if you want to get something to eat. I've got a lot to think over."

Now, even though we have gotten him safely back to his room, I find I am not wild about leavin' him alone.

"Oh, we already ate," I sez. "So we'll just . . ."

I realize at this point that I am talkin' to the door, which the Boss has just shut in my face.

". . . Set fire to the palace and roast a couple hot dogs," I finish with a grimace.

"See what I mean?" Nunzio sez. "This is the way it's been around here since you left for your assignment. Sometimes he talks your ear off, and then the next time you see him, it's like you don't exist."

"He does seem a little distracted," I sez.

"A little distracted?" Nunzio shoots back. "If he was any more out of it, he wouldn't know if he was wearing his clothes backward."

"Check me on this, cuz," I sez, ignorin' his attempts at humor. "Have you ever seen anyone so upset just after pickin' up their pay?"

"Not really, now that you mention it," he sez, frownin' slightly. "It was like something about getting paid upset him. You think maybe they shorted him with extra deductions?"

"C'mon, Nunzio," I sez. "Who's gonna short him? The Queen is tryin' to get him to marry her and Grimble is scared to death of him. Besides, did you see the size of that bag? He could barely carry it. That sure didn't look like a short payday to me."

"Well, something has him upset," Nunzio sez. "Maybe Grimble said something to him that hit him wrong."

We was still talkin' about this when the Boss opens his door.

"Guido! Nunzio!" he sez. "Come in here for a second."

We follow him into the room, and he sits down at his desk, the sack with his pay in it still on the desktop in front of him.

"I've got a little assignment for you boys," he sez with a smile.

"Sure, Boss," we say together.

"But first, I want to check something. As long as I've known you, you've both made it clear that, in the past, you've had no qualms about bending the rules as situations called for it—working outside the law, as it were. Is that correct?"

"That's right."

"No problem."

"All right. The job I have for you is to be done secretly, without anybody knowing that I'm behind it. Not even Aahz or Bunny. Understand?"

Now, this does not sound good. I haven't been all that happy keepin' the real reason for my investigations from the Boss, but him includin' me and Nunzio in secrets he is keepin' from Aahz and the rest of the team is downright creepy.

Still, I hide my discomfort and nod.

"Okay. Here's the job," he sez, pushin' the bag forward. "I want you to take this money and get rid of it."

To say the least, this is an unusual concept. I sneak a peek at Nunzio to see how he's reactin', only to find him lookin' back at me.

"I don't quite get you, Boss," I sez, careful-like. "What do you want us to do with it?"

"I don't care and I don't want to know," he sez. "I just want this money back in circulation within the kingdom. Spend it or give it to charity. Better still, figure some way of passing it around to those people who have been complaining that they can't pay their taxes."

I am extremely confused at this. I look openly at Nunzio for help, but he just shrugs.

"I dunno, Boss," I sez finally. "It don't seem right, somehow. I mean, we're supposed to be collectin' taxes from people . . . not givin' it to them."

"What Guido means," Nunzio sez, "is that our speciality is extractin' funds from people and institutions. Givin' it back is a little out of our line."

"Well then I guess it's about time you expanded your horizons," the Boss sez, firm-like. "Anyway, that's the assignment. Understand?"

There's only one acceptable answer to that.

"Yes, Boss," we sez together, but not real enthusiastic.

"And remember, not a word about this to the rest of the team."

"If you say so, Boss."

I pick up the bag with my good hand. It is impressively heavy, and I decide to give it one more try.

"Ummm . . . Are you sure you want to do this, Boss?" I sez. "It don't seem right, somehow. Most folks would have to work for a lifetime to earn this much money."

"That's the point," he sez, almost to himself.

"Huh?"

"Never mind," he sez. "I'm sure. Now do it. Okay?"

"Consider it done."

Neither of us said anything until we were back in Nunzio's room, each of us lost in his own thoughts. Once we were there, I dropped the sack of gold onto his bed and plopped down in a chair.

Nunzio remained standin'.

"Okay," he sez, breakin' the silence. "So what do you think?"

"I think we gotta find a couple money belts or saddle bags or somethin' to carry that gold around," I sez. "Haulin' it in that bag is not only an open invitation to trouble, it's hard on the back."

"That's it?" Nunzio sez, his squeaky voice climbin' an octave. "With everything that's happening, all you can think about is your back?"

"What do you want me to say?" I snaps back at him. "That the Boss has gone round the bend? That he's so far gone in foo-foo land that he'd need a map to find his way back?"

"Well, yeah," Nunzio sez, taken a bit aback by my outburst. "He is, isn't he?"

"That's so obvious, it goes without sayin'," I sez, droppin' my voice back to normal. "I mean, really. 'Give the money away.' No wonder he wanted us to keep it secret. If Aahz found out, he'd have a heart attack on the spot."

"So, what are we supposed to do?"

"Do?" I sez. "Didn't you hear? We're supposed to take his pay and re-distribute it to the needy."

"But that's crazy!!"

"So what's your point?" I sez. "How long have you worked for the Mob? You're gonna try to tell me you've never had to take orders from a crazy person before?"

"C'mon, Guido," Nunzio sez. "It's Skeeve we're talking about here. Not some power-hungry Mob underboss."

Now this is truly an indication of how upset my cousin is. In all the years we've worked together, this is the first time I've known him to lose his professionalism to a point where he referred to our immediate superior by his proper name rather than the generic phrase 'the Boss.' That meant that he was so fond of Skeeve as a person that he was forgettin' to maintain that emotional distance necessary for someone in our line of work. Unfortunately, he wasn't the only one.

"I know what you mean, cousin," I sez, quiet-like. "The trouble is, I don't see as where we have a lot of options right now. I mean, what can we do? If we ignore this assignment, then we're goin' against a direct order. If we try to alert the rest of the team as to what's goin' on with Skeeve, then we're goin' against his direct orders to keep it a secret. Besides, I've got a hunch that they already know how close Skeeve is to losin' it. Most of them have known him better and for a lot longer than we have."

We look at each other in silence for a few moments.

"I guess that brings us to my original question," Nunzio sez with a sigh. "What are we gonna do?"

"What we always do," I sez. "We're gonna follow orders. Of course, if we clear up a few of the Boss's other problems at the same time, that'll just be a bonus. Right?"

"That sounds like you've got an idea, cuz," Nunzio sez, cockin' an eyebrow at me.

"As a matter of fact, I do," I sez, showin' a few extra teeth in a smile. "When it comes to passin' money back to the populace, I think I know just the crew to help us. The fact that they're currently on our list as problem children just makes it all the sweeter."

I manage to appear confident enough that by the time I get done outlinin' what I have in mind, Nunzio is smilin', too.

What I manage to keep hidden from him is my real worry about the current situation. However it all comes out in the end, my readin' of this convoluted job and the effect it's havin' on Skeeve and the rest of the team is that we'll never again be able to get back to how we were before.

FIFTEEN

"You're sure about this?" I sez, starin' at the sporting goods shop.

"As sure as one can be about anything without a full confession," Pookie sez.

It occurs to me that I could tell her a thing or two about confessions, but I let it pass. Such discussions would only confuse the issues at hand.

We were back at the Sherwood Arms subdivision, where Nunzio and I caught up with Pookie, Spyder, and Chumley. While I couldn't tell them the exact nature of our assignment from the Boss, I felt it was necessary to let them know we was in the area, just so's we didn't look suspicious if we ran into them by accident. All I said was things was heatin' up back at the palace, and that it would be best if we could conclude our business with the bandits in the forest ASAP so's we could get back and give the Boss our undivided attention. Chumley gave me a bit of the fish-eye, but Pookie and Spyder bought the explanation without question.

As it turned out, however, they had developed a solid lead on the bandits.

"Tell me again how you figured this out," I sez.

"Actually, it was Spyder who came up with it," Pookie sez. "Why don't you explain it, little sister?"

"It was nothing, really," Spyder sez. "I got to thinking about the fact that they were attacking the tax collectors with bows. Unless you're real good with one of those things, that means a lot of arrows, and unless you're big on making the things yourself, that means a supply source. Remember how many crossbow bolts we had on stock when we were running the supply depot?"

I just nodded and gestured for her to continue.

"Well, I did a little checking around, and it seems the only place that stocks arrows in quantity in these parts is that shop you were in the first time we were here."

"That would explain why that guy was so closed-mouthed when you leaned on him, Guido," Pookie put in. "If he's making money supplying the bandits, the last thing he would want would be for us to shut them down."

"There's more to it than that," Spyder sez. "We've been keeping a watch on the place and there's about half a dozen guys who are in and out of there all the time. They aren't purchasing or delivering anything. It's like they're meeting or getting assignments or something."

"You're sure they haven't spotted you staking the place out?" Nunzio sez.

"Not a chance, old boy," Chumley puts in. "We've been taking turns and using disguise spells to alter our appearance. They're blissfully ignorant that we're onto them."

"They got any kind of a schedule on these meetin's?" I sez.

"Nothing regular," Pookie sez. "But there's a bunch of them in there right now."

That's all I need to hear.

"Well, Nunzio," I sez, settling my weapons on my belt, "let's you and me wander over there and have a little chat with them."

"You want some help or any kind of disguises?" Pookie sez.

"I think we'll play this as a come-as-you-are-party," I sez. "The rest of you stay out of sight for now. If our play doesn't work, it'll be your turn next."

"Are you sure this is such a good idea? Us taking them on with just the two of us?" Nunzio sez to me under his breath as we cross the streets.

"It may not be the best play," I sez, "but it's the only way we can play it without lettin' the others know about the orders we got from the Boss."

"When he told us to give away the gold, I don't think he meant we should have people take it off our corpses," Nunzio points out.

"Relax, cousin," I sez. "You'll see. This is strictly amateur hour. These suburb guys are even softer than the city-street types we're used to leanin' on. Just run the standard hard stare on 'em and we shouldn't have any problems. Here we go."

Now, there are two ways of flexin' one's muscles when bracin' a person or place: hard, and soft. The first time I hit this place with Pookie and Spyder, we was usin' the 'soft' technique. That is, we talked soft, smiled a lot, and handled things gentle, all of which emphasized the fact that we could have been a lot rougher if we chose.

Now, I figured it was time to use the 'hard' approach.

Standin' in front of the door, I take a deep breath, then raise my arms and slap it hard with both hands. Said door responds by flyin' open noisily. (The fact that it stays on its hinges is a tribute to its solid construction rather than an indication that I'm losin' my strength.) Before the sound dies away, I walk through the resultin' openin' with Nunzio crowdin' close behind me.

If there is any doubt in my mind as to whether Pookie is correct in her deductions, it is dispelled by the reactions of the guys inside. The whole group freezes in place, and in general look about guilty as gamblers in a protected bookie joint when an unbought cop walks in.

The guy I talked to on my first visit is behind the counter, and I fix him with a hard stare.

"Remember me?" I sez.

"Umm . . . Sure. You're the guy who was in here before with a couple . . . friends. Right?" he stammers.

"Close, but no cigar," I sez, makin my way slowly up to the assemblage. "I'm the guy you was gonna find out some information for. Information about the bandits in the forest. Ring a bell?"

"Umm . . . We'll be going now, Robb," one of the guys in the shop sez, edgin' toward the door.

"I don't think so," I sez. "Nunzio!"

"Got 'em, Guido," my cousin sez, leanin' in the doorway.

The group of guys looks at him, then take up a position as far as they can get from either Nunzio or myself.

I turns back to the guy behind the counter.

"You was about to say?"

"Uh . . . Of course," he sez, backin' away from the counter. "I've done some asking around, and . . ."

"From what I've heard, you wouldn't have had to ask to far now, would you?" I sez, leanin' on the counter and showin' a few teeth. "Like, no farther than who's standin' in this shop right now. Am I right?"

"Well . . . um . . ." the guy stammers.

I hold up a hand to silence him.

"Before you say anythin'," I sez. "Let's be sure we understand each other. Now, by this time you have figured out that, in our line of work, my colleague and I occasionally have to hurt people. Right?"

He nods vigorously.

"That's part of the job, and we do it. Nothin' personal." I leans in a little closer. "If, however, said hurtee has insulted my intelligence by lyin' to me, then it makes me mad and I do take it personally. Know what I mean?"

The guy swallows hard, then nods again.

"Now, keepin' that in mind, let's continue the conversation. I was sayin' that you wouldn't have to ask further than the guys here in the shop to get information about the bandits in the forest, and you was about to agree. Right?"

The guy looks at his friends, then he looks at Nunzio and me, then drops his eyes and nods.

"I didn't quite hear that," I sez.

The guy nods more vigorously.

I look over at Nunzio, who kind of shrugs helplessly.

This could take a while. Unfortunately, we don't have whole bunches of time. If we don't settle this quick, the other team members are gonna come lookin' for us.

"Tell you what . . . Robb, is it?" I sez. "What say I just tell you what's been goin' on, and you just point out any parts that I get wrong. Okay?"

Again, the weak nod.

"First off, we know you and your buddies here are involved with the bandits," I sez. "Whether this here is the whole gang or you're just a part of it doesn't matter right now. For our purposes, you're it. Right?"

Swallow and nod.

"What's more," I sez, "the way we've got it figured, you've been usin' part of the loot to pay off the locals hereabouts so they'll cover for you."

"No, we haven't," the guy sez, finally findin' his voice.

"Excuse me?" I sez, cockin' an eyebrow at him.

"Paying off the locals, I mean," he sez, quick-like. "I won't say it isn't a good idea, but it never occurred to us. We've been keeping it all."

This presents a problem. I mean, our whole idea of lookin' these jokers up is to use them to redistribute the Boss's gold. Clearly I am gonna have to think of a way to revise our plan whilst in mid-negotiation.

"Whatever," I sez. "Now, what we're lookin' for here is a plan so's we can all eat out of the same bowl. Like, say, maybe we finance your operation in exchange for a small percentage of the take."

"Don't do it, Robb."

The guy now talkin' is a skinny, red-headed dude who

is suddenly lookin' very serious instead of scared.

"Why not, Will?" sez Robb. "It could be the perfect solution to our . . . predicament."

"It would be putting our head in a noose," the redhead sez. "So far, all they have is hearsay. If we accept money from them, then it's a clear admission of what we're doing, and they'll have grounds to arrest us. If we try to say that we were just kidding, then they can nail us for fraud. Either way, taking their money would be a bad idea."

It occurs to me that this guy is soundin' a lot like a lawyer, which is a whole different sub-species of bandit than the type I had been figurin' on dealin' with.

"And what about the Game Preserve?" puts in another of the group.

"What about it?" I sez, now thoroughly confused.

"You know, the plans to sell the Royal Game Preserve off to the lumber companies," he sez.

"What plans?" I sez. "You know anything about this, Nunzio?"

"It's news to me," Nunzio sez. "Sounds like the kind of thing that Grimble would come up with, though. Odds are the Boss doesn't even know about it, what with all the stuff they've been having him sign."

"There! You see! I knew it!" the red-head chimes in. "These guys are working for the kingdom. This whole act has been nothing but a sting operation. It's a clear case of entrapment."

This meetin' has gotten completely out of control. It comes to me that there is only one way out of this mess.

"Shaddup, alla youse!" I bellow.

Everybody freezes and looks at me.

"I am hereby declarin' all of youse to be members of the Sherwood Arms Grievance Committee. What's more," I pause to give them all a smile, "your first duty is to accompany us back to the Royal Palace so's you can present your problems to the Boss . . . I mean, the Great Skeeve personally."

SIXTEEN

Surprisingly enough, the trip back to the palace is extremely pleasant.

We have allowed the Sherwood Arms delegation to keep their bows, just to prove to them that they are not bein' arrested, and once they loosen up, they prove to be the nicest travelin' companions one could ask for. They are always chatterin' back and forth with jokes and stories about their huntin' trips and life in the suburbs, and one of them is actually some sort of entertainer who fills in the low spots with songs and stand-up comedy routines.

Then, too, there is the ongoin' archery contest. From the get-go, they are fascinated by the custom mini-crossbows that Nunzio and I are carryin', which in no time develops into a shootin' match, with us pickin' targets at random on the road ahead to aim at as we walk. This is really no contest at all, as the Nunzio and I can easily outshoot any of them, even when we rigs the match a bit by shootin' first so that by the time they take their turn, the targets are considerably closer. Finally, we end

up passin' our weapons to Spyder and Pookie, but even
then the match is one-sided. Once they get the hang of
the hair-triggers, they are also makin' the delegates look
bad. Fortunately, the Sherwood boys don't take offense
at this. In fact, they take to cheerin' the good shots and
needlin' each other when they miss.

"I say, old boy," Chumley sez, fallin' in step with me
as we walk. He, like Pookie, is still usin' a disguise spell
to make him look like a local so as not to spook our
guests. "Do you really think this is such a good idea? I
mean, the whole point of this exercise has been to investigate and handle the situation without bothering Skeeve.
Now, we're effectively bringing it back and dumping it
in his lap unannounced."

This question, and variations on it, has been the most
popular subject of conversation among the team since I
decided to bring the bandits back to the palace to meet
the Boss. Every one of them, as we were travelin', has
pulled me aside out of earshot of the delegation to ask, in
varyin' degrees of politeness, if I know what I am doin'.

"I figure it's our best shot to straighten out this mess,"
I sez. "These boys have it in their head that the Boss is
some kind of power-mad monster who's out to take the
kingdom away from the Queen. Now, you know the Boss.
Do you really think that anyone can talk to him for more
than a few minutes and still keep that impression?"

"He's likeable enough, all right," Chumley sez. "But
he can have a bit of a temper, too. I just hope we catch
him in a good mood. Oh well. I guess we're committed
now. We'll just have to muddle through somehow."

This is not exactly the enthusiastic vote of confidence
I had been hopin' for from Chumley. He is probably the
most level-headed member of our team, despite his bein'
a Troll, and his worries do nothin' toward givin' me peace
of mind.

"Okay, cuz," Nunzio sez, slidin' into Chumley's place

as that notable drops back to talk to Pookie. "Now that we're almost there, how do you figure we should play this, exactly?"

We are makin' our final approach to the palace, so the time for analyzin' and plannin' is over. It's now time to settle on specifics.

"I figure we take them into the courtyard," I sez. "Then, you and the others hold 'em there and keep them amused while I hunt up the Boss. I'll give him a quick run-down on what's happenin', then bring him out to meet the delegates."

"You're gonna explain all this to the Boss?" he sez, raisin' an eyebrow. "Are you sure you don't want me to handle that little task?"

"It's nice of you to offer, cuz," I sez. "But I figure this is my job. I know you're better at talkin' and explainin' than I am, but this whole investigation, and particularly bringin' the delegation to the palace, was my idea. If the Boss is gonna blow his stack and take it out on someone, it should be me."

"Okay," he sez with a sigh, clappin' a hand on my shoulder. "I just hope you know what you're doing."

The repetition of this theme is startin' to get on my nerves. You see, I don't really know what I'm doin'. I've just come up with what I think is the best solution and am keepin' my fingers crossed. Now, as we are enterin' the passage to the courtyard, I am feelin' less and less confident that this is a good idea.

"So, Guido," Robb sez, edgin' up to me. "What are we supposed to say to the Skeeve, anyway? I mean, I don't think any of us have actually met a real magician before. Is there any kind of protocol we should follow?"

"Just relax and be yourselves," I sez. "At first, let Nunzio and me do most of the talkin'. Then just talk to him like you would anybody else."

"Is there any kind of special way we should address him? Like 'Your Greatness' or anything?"

"You aren't listenin' to me, Robb," I sez, gettin' a little exasperated. "The Boss is a nice guy. In fact, he's younger than you are. All you have to do is . . ."

"Hey Guido! What's up?"

I look up to find Aahz wavin' and walkin' towards us across the courtyard.

I start to wave back, then realize that Robb is startin' to fumble with his bow.

"What are you doin'?" I sez.

"That's a demon!" Robb sez, his eyes all wild-like.

The rest of the delegation is also startin' to load arrows, and I realize that we have not completely briefed them as to the sights and sounds they could expect to encounter when they reached the palace.

"Hey! Relax!" I sez, hastily. "That's just Aahz. He's the Boss's partner, and . . ."

"Gleep!"

Around the corner comes Gleep. Apparently Aahz was exercising him in the courtyard when we arrived. In a flash, I can see we've got trouble.

"That's a dragon!!"

"Relax, everybody!!" I bellows in my best command voice. "There's no need to . . ."

Just then, Gleep catches sight of Nunzio and comes boundin' forward.

"Gleep!"

That's when it all hits the fan.

A lot of things happen so fast that I am left with a confusin' array of separate images.

-The bows come up loaded with arrows.

-Aahz stops in his tracks.

-Gleep slams on the brakes and throws himself sideways in front of Aahz.

-Pookie and Spyder pile into the delegation, tryin' to stop them from shootin'.

-An arrow flies and . . .

Gleep gives out a high-pitch wail, rears up, and then collapses on his side.

At the sound, everybody freezes in place and stares in silence, like we was all in a picture for one of those play advertisements.

Then, everyone starts talkin' at once.

"What did you do that for??!!"

"But it was attacking!"

"No it wasn't! It wanted to play!"

"That's Skeeve's pet you just shot!"

"Oh geez!"

"How were we supposed to know?"

While the babble is goin' on behind me, I runs forward and joins Aahz, who is kneelin' by Gleep.

"How is he?" I sez.

Even as I speak, I realize this is a kinda stupid question. From where I stand, I can see the arrow stickin' out of the Boss's pet just behind his front leg. For a crew that normally couldn't hit the broadside of a barn if they was inside, this time they managed to come up with a shot that was deadly accurate.

"It's not good," Aahz sez, not lookin' up. "You better have someone get Skeeve."

"Nunzio!" I call. "Get the Boss! Quick!"

"Gleep," the dragon sez, tryin' weakly to raise its head.

"Just lie quiet, fellah," Aahz sez, in a surprisingly gentle voice. "Skeeve will be here soon."

I turn and walk back to where the delegation is now huddled together.

"Robb," I sez, beckonin' him forward."

"Geez, Guido," he sez. "We didn't know . . ."

"Shaddup!" I sez, cuttin' him short. "Remember what I told you about talkin' with the Boss?"

"Yeah?"

"Well, forget it. With what's just happened, you better let Nunzio and me do all the talkin'."

It seems like it takes forever, but it's probably not more than a minute or two before Nunzio and the Boss come flyin' out of the palace. Of course, in the Boss's case, this is literal type statement. That is to say, Nunzio is leadin' the way at a pace a few notches short of a dead run, while the Boss is floatin' along just behind him. Even at this distance, I can see that he's lookin' happier than I have seen him in a long time.

This surprises me.

Not that he is flyin'. That is one of the smaller magiks that he has at his disposal, even though he doesn't use it all that much. Rather, I am surprised that he seems happy, as I can see nothin' in the current state of affairs that would put him in such a mood.

Then he sees Gleep and he stops smilin'. At this, I realize what has happened. Nunzio has simply fetched him without tellin' him what was up. Any hopes I have for his bein' in a good mood disappear along with his smile.

In a flash he is on the ground and kneelin' at Gleep's side, cradlin' his pet's head in his arms.

"What's wrong, fellah?" I hear him say. "Aahz? What's the matter with him?"

Aahz glances at us, then clears his throat.

"Skeeve, I . . ." he begins, then stops as the Boss suddenly stiffens up.

He has just noticed the arrow that's stickin' out of Gleep's side. An expression dances across his face that does not bode well for any of us in the near vicinity.

Just then, Gleep stirs again, raisin' his head.

"Take it easy, fellah," the Boss sez, his expression softenin' again.

Gleep cranks his head around and looks the Boss in the eye.

"Skeeve?" he sez, then goes limp.

The Boss carefully puts Gleep's head on the ground, then gets up and stands lookin' at him for a minute. Then he looks at us.

In my work with the Mob, I have met several people who could threaten you with just a look. I've even done it myself when the situation called for it. But in all my years, I have never seem anything like the look the Boss is givin' us right now.

"All right," he sez in a deadly-soft voice. "I want to know what's been going on here . . . and I want to know now!!"

Remember when I said that when Nunzio went lookin' for the Boss, it seemed to take a lot longer than it actually did? Well, it seemed even longer this time before anyone spoke . . . practically years.

Finally, Aahz broke the silence.

"Um . . . partner?" he sez.

"Not now, Aahz," the Boss sez, still starin' at us.

"Suit yourself," Aahz shrugs. "I just thought you might want to take care of Gleep before getting in to all this."

The Boss's head comes around with a snap.

"Take care of Gleep?" he sez. "But isn't he . . . ? I mean . . ."

Aahz frowns at him for a second, then his expression clears.

"Oh! I get it now. You thought . . ." he breaks off with a little chuckle. "Relax, partner. He'll be fine. He just passed out from the shock is all."

"But the arrow . . . ?"

"Dragons are tough." Aahz smiles. "Besides, most people don't know much about dragon anatomy. That arrow's nowhere near where his heart is. Once we get it out of him, he should heal up fine."

Now, I'll admit that I am among those that Aahz is referrin' to that don't know anything about dragon anatomy. This does not, however, mean that I am slow on the uptake.

"Nunzio!" I barks. "Find Massha fast. Tell her to bring that stuff she used on my arm. Spyder! Scout around for a wagon big enough that we can move Gleep back to the stables. If anyone gives you any grief, convince them. Either that or tell 'em to take it up with me later."

In the blink of an eye, they are both up and runnin'.

"Can I help out at all?" sez one of the delegates, steppin' up to me.

"Like how?" I sez, frownin' as I try to remember the guy's name. "You're . . ."

"Tuck," he sez. "I'm a cook. I heard the . . . the green gentleman say something about cutting the arrow out. Well, I'm pretty good with a knife and know a bit about animal anatomy . . . though not about dragons specifically . . . and . . ."

"Okay, stand by," I sez. "Just don't do anything until Massha gets here."

"Massha?" he sez.

"Don't worry. You'll know her when you see her."

After that, it was pretty much routine. Tuck was as good as his word and got the arrow out of the Boss's pet with minimal blood bein' spilled. Massha was right there with her magik salve, and by the time we got around to loadin' Gleep onto the wagon, the wound was already healin'.

I was takin' a breather after helpin' with the latter chore, Gleep bein' no featherweight, when Robb beckons me aside for a quick chat.

"Guido," he sez, "the boys and I are going to take couple rooms at that inn we passed just outside the castle.

Things are crazy enough right now I think our business with Skeeve can wait until tomorrow."

"You're probably right," I sez. "It's kind of a shame, though. Your havin' to wait after havin' come all this way to meet the Boss."

"Oh, the actual meeting is more of a formality now," he sez. "I'm sure we'll be able to work out some kind of an arrangement with him. I'd say your point has definitely been proven."

"Which point is that?" I sez, genuinely puzzled.

"About how Skeeve is a nice guy and more reasonable than we gave him credit for. I mean, talk is easy and the best of us can get fooled, but that was a pretty solid demonstration we got." He paused and shook his head. "The kid was genuinely upset about his dragon getting shot, and deservedly so, I might add. He really wanted to lay into us, and no one could have or would have stopped him. Still, even when he was deadly-eyed mad, his first reaction was to ask for an explanation . . . to hear our side of what had happened. Then, when it turned out that the dragon was just wounded, his main concern was taking care of his pet, not going after punishment or vengeance. To me, that makes him a hell of a man."

"That's the Boss, all right," I sez, grinnin' slightly.

"Yeah, well you can also tell a lot about a man by the friends he attracts," Robb smiles. "Even though your crew is pretty fearsome when viewed from the outside, it's also easy to see that you're all fiercely loyal to Skeeve . . . far beyond a simple employee-employer relationship. It speaks well of him, and you."

Before I can say anything in response to this, he sticks out his hand. I shake it, and he turns and marches off to rejoin the rest of the delegation.

As I am watchin' him go, I suddenly realize there is someone standin' next to me.

"Oh. Hi, Boss," I sez.

"Guido," he acknowledges. "I believe you were about to explain to me what's going on. Let's take a walk and you can fill me in."

So I do.

I tell him everything we've been doin' since he got back from Perv, with only a little bit of editin' for content.

When I get done, he is silent for a long time.

"I'm sorry, Boss," I sez, finally, tryin' to prod him into commentin'.

"No, Guido," he sez, quiet-like. "I'm the one who's sorry."

With that, he walks off in the direction of the stables.

SEVENTEEN

> *"Some of my best friends are dragons."*
> **SIEGFRIED**

Skeeve the Great. What a joke.

If there was ever a time in my life when I felt less great than now, it has been mercifully forgotten.

The irony was that not that long ago, barely an hour really, I had been on top of the world. I had told Queen Hemlock that I didn't want to marry her and survived the experience. Not only survived it, but had also escaped the awful threat of her abdicating and leaving me to run the kingdom by myself. For the first time in months, I was completely free from obligations and commitments. I had been literally walking on air.

Then Gleep got shot. To boot, that led to my finding out that there was a whole batch of problems the team had been handling without even telling me about them. Handling, as in putting themselves in the line of fire so I wouldn't be bothered.

It was disturbing to realize that I couldn't trust the team anymore. At least, I felt like I couldn't trust them because they didn't trust me enough to be open and honest about things anymore.

I was feeling confused and more than a little hurt, so I did what I usually do when things start crowding in on me. I retreated to the stables to hang out with Gleep.

Of course now, he was sleeping. Recovering from shock while his wound healed, Massha had said. I glanced over to be sure he was resting quietly, then went back to thinking.

The nice thing about the stables is that few people ever came here. I've been told that it's the smell that keeps them away, but when you've spent years with a pet dragon whose eating habits give him bad breath that would gag a maggot, it takes more than a bit of barnyard perfume to bother you. As a result, I had a place to go where I could be alone. A place where no one would intrude. A place where . . .

"Hi, Skeeve."

The voice was easily recognizable, so I didn't even look around.

"Okay, you found me, Bunny," I said, heaving a sigh. "What is it now? More spreadsheets? Did Grimble misplace a decimal in the budget?"

She didn't answer, so I finally turned to face her.

As always, she was a delightfully curvaceous bundle who is a delight to look at. Now, however, she was staring at the ground and trembling slightly.

"Actually," she said softly, "I came down to see how Gleep was. I really didn't mean to intrude. I'll leave you alone and check back later."

She turned and started to leave.

"Whoa. Wait a minute, Bunny," I called. "I'm sorry. I didn't mean to snap at you. It's just . . . it's been a rough day. That's all."

She stopped, but didn't turn back.

"So, so you want me to leave or not?" she said.

"Yes. No. I don't know," I stammered. "I'm so turned around . . . I just don't know."

"That's really the heart of the problem, isn't it?" she said, turning at last. "If you don't know what you want, how is anyone else supposed to figure it out?"

"It's more than that," I said. "I just don't know who to trust anymore."

"What, you mean because of the little side project Guido and Nunzio took on without telling you?"

"You heard about that, huh?" I said, then a thought struck me. "Or did you know about it all along? Have you been part of this conspiracy of silence the whole time?"

"As a matter of fact, I didn't know about it," she said. "I guess they weren't sure that I wouldn't have felt obligated to tell you."

"That's a relief," I sighed.

"Is it?" she said. "I'll be honest with you, Skeeve. If they had included me in their planning, I would have gone along with it."

"You would?"

"Yes, I would," she said. "This whole thing with Queen Hemlock and the kingdom's finances has had you tied in knots, Skeeve. You really didn't need any other distractions."

"I see," I said. "I would have thought, if anyone, that you would be on my side, Bunny."

"When did it become 'sides,' Skeeve?" Bunny sighed. "We're all supposed to be on the same team. Remember?"

"Well, yes. But . . ."

"Have you listened to yourself lately, Skeeve?" she continued. "When I first walked in here, you nearly bit my head off because you thought I was coming to you with more problems. Now, in the same conversation, you're upset because Guido and Nunzio didn't come to you with new problems. You think you're confused?

Well, don't feel all alone. The whole team is confused right now."

"I don't . . . I just can't seem to get a fix on things anymore," I said.

"I've noticed," she said, turning to go. "Well, when you sort things out, or if you want someone to talk to, let me know. Until then, I think I'll just try to stay out of your way."

"Bunny, I . . ." I started to say, but she had already gone.

Terrific.

I leaned against Gleep's stall and let my thoughts whirl through my mind.

Now, on top of everything else, Bunny was upset with me. It was strange to realize just how much that bothered me. When her uncle, Don Bruce, first assigned her to me as my moll, she had come on so strong that she made me uneasy just to be around. Heck, she scared the pants off me. Since then, she had settled into the role of administrative assistant and personal confidante, performing with such competence and efficiency that she was now an indispensable member of the team. I had nothing but the highest respect for her, and wanted desperately for her to respect me in turn.

"Bunny . . . right."

I looked up to find Gleep awake and staring at me.

"Gleep!" I said. "Are you all right, fellah? You're looking better and . . . you're talking?"

I remembered now that, just before he collapsed, he had said my name, effectively doubling his vocabulary up until that point. I had been impressed at the time, but now . . .

"Bunny . . . right," he said again.

"Wait a minute, Gleep," I said. "You can talk? Why haven't you said anything before?"

"Secret," he said, then craned his neck to look toward the door. "Keep . . . secret?"

"Sure, I'll keep it a secret," I said. "But . . . wait a minute. What do you mean 'Bunny's right'?"

"Friends . . . love . . . Skeeve," my pet said. "Skeeve . . . not . . . happy. Friends . . . try . . . make . . . happy. Not . . . know . . . how."

Maybe it was his broken speech or the simplification it required, but what Gleep was saying made sense. It kind of summarized what a lot of people had been telling me. In an absence of information from me, the team had been left to their own devices at interpreting what it would take to make me happy, then acting on those interpretations. In turn, I had been looking at those actions without realizing what they were doing, and . . .

"Wait a minute, Gleep," I said. "Those 'accidents' you've been having. Did they have anything to do with what you're telling me now?"

"Gleep," he said, chewing at his foot.

"Oh no," I said. "The 'dumb animal' bit won't work any more. Answer the question."

He looked at me levelly.

"Skeeve . . . not . . . happy," he said. "Gleep . . . love . . . Skeeve."

If I thought my brain was whirling before, now it was doing loop-the-loops.

"But Gleep, I don't know what it will take to make me happy," I said desperately.

"Talk . . . Aahz," he said.

"What?"

"Talk . . . Aahz," he repeated. "Aahz . . . help."

Actually, that was pretty good advice. Aahz had been my teacher and mentor long before he took me as a full partner. Not only had he seen a lot and been around for a long time, he had a vested interest in my well-being.

"Good idea, Gleep," I said. "But now that we're talking . . ."

"Talk . . . Aahz," he said again. "Gleep . . . sleep . . . now. Hurt."

With that, he lowered his head to the ground, heaved a sigh, and closed his eyes.

Having been effectively dismissed by my own pet, I went to find Aahz.

I was so caught up in my thoughts that I barely noticed my surroundings as I made my way through the palace courtyard. Even though I wasn't seeing things, however, didn't mean others weren't seeing me.

"Hi, Skeeve. How's the dragon?"

It was Pookie, leaning against the courtyard wall in the shadows.

"Gleep? Oh, I think he'll be fine, Pookie. Thanks for asking."

"Any chance you have a minute to talk?" she said. "I know you're busy, but . . ."

She let it trail off.

"Sure, if you don't mind talking while we walk," I said. "What's up?"

"I wanted to talk to you now that things have calmed down a little," she said, falling in step with me. "Is what I've heard right? The whole thing with the Queen has been resolved?"

"That's right," I said, forcing a smile. "I'm off the hook. It turns out that her whole threat to abdicate and stick me with Possiltum if I didn't marry her was just a bluff. I'm still single, and she's going to handle the kingdom."

"Uh-huh," she said. "Well, in that case it seems like it's time for me to move on."

"It does?" I said, slowing slightly.

Truth to tell, with all the excitement that had been goin on, I really hadn't given much thought to Pookie and her continued employment. Apparently she had.

"Sure," she said. "I was only hanging around because there was some question as to how the Queen would take it if you turned her down. Now that we've cleared that hurdle, I can't see anything for me to do around here that can't be handled by Guido and Nunzio."

"I dunno, Pookie," I said. "I haven't had a chance to talk with the rest of the team, but I'm pretty sure they'd be interested in taking you on as a full-time member of M.Y.T.H. Inc. At this point, I don't think there's any question as to your being qualified."

"I've thought of that," she said. "No offense, but I don't really think it's for me. I still get too much of a kick freelancing through the dimensions to settle down to steady work just now. Besides, I've got a new partner now. I'd want to teach her the ropes a bit and get her some seasoning before she'd be ready to apply for a place in your crew."

I homed in on two phrases in her statement: 'new partner' and 'her/she.' Pookie hadn't met all that many people here on Klah, much less female people. Massha was about to get married, and Queen Hemlock wasn't budging. By elimination, it sounded like she was talking about Bunny.

"A new partner?" I said, trying to make it sound casual. "Anyone I know?"

"Don't know how well you know her," Pookie said. "But it's Spyder, if that's what you're asking."

I felt strangely relieved that she wasn't referring to Bunny, but her answer still left me puzzled.

"Spyder?" I said, frowning. "The guy from the Army that's been checking on the tax collecters? He's a woman? I mean . . ."

"I guess you don't know her too well," Pookie said with

a laugh. "Trust me, Skeeve. She's a woman. I know the difference."

"So, you're teaming with her now," I said quickly, try-ing to hide my embarrassment. "When did this happen?"

"Well, we've been working together on the tax collec-tors getting hijacked, and we hit it off pretty well," she said. "The kid's a little wet behind the ears, but there's plenty of potential there if anyone's willing to take the time to work with her."

For some reason, that reminded me of my early days with Aahz. As complex as things had become lately, I found myself reflecting on those times with a certain amount of nostalgia.

"Well, if your mind's made up, I don't see where I can object," I said. "Any idea how soon you'll be leaving?"

"It'll take a day or two to get her sprung from the Army," Pookie said, "but after that we can pretty much pick our time. The nice thing about being on your own is that you can name your own schedule."

"Just be sure to stop by and say 'Goodbye' before you go," I said. "If nothing else, I think you're due an extra bonus this round."

"That's sweet of you, Skeeve," she smiled. "But then, you've been a square-shooter all along. In case it doesn't get said later, I'll miss you. It's been a real experience."

With that she turned and headed off in the opposite direction.

Even though we hadn't worked together that long or that closely, I felt a certain loss thinking of her eventual departure. She had been part of the team, and it wouldn't be the same without her.

Of course, Massha would be leaving as well, now that she was getting married.

It made me wonder what other changes might be in store now that our work in Possiltum was finished.

EIGHTEEN

"I was hoping for a little fatherly advice."

J. CHRIST

"C'mon in, partner," Aahz said, beckoning me into his room. "I was wondering if you were going to stop by."

That was all the invitation I needed, and, after casually closing the door behind me, sank into one of room's chairs.

"Would you like something to drink, or are you still on the wagon?"

I had been making an effort to cut back on my drinking, but right now a drink sounded like a good idea.

"Some wine would be nice, thanks," I said.

"Coming right up," he said, moving to the tray containing several earthen bottles of wine and goblets that he always seemed to have in his room. "So. How's Gleep doing?"

"He seems to be healing up incredibly fast," I said. "That stuff Massha used on the wound is amazingly effective."

"Don't forget, dragons are tough," Aahz said, handing me a goblet of wine. "They heal fast even without magical aid. On the whole, they're smart, too. Did I mention that when that yahoo let fly with his bow, that Gleep actually jumped in front of me? For all I know, he might have saved my life by taking that arrow."

"I didn't know that."

"Well, take it from me, he did," Aahz grimaced, shaking his head slightly. "You know, it makes me feel a little bad. I mean, I've been making snide comments about that beast ever since you got him, and then he goes and jumps in front of me when the shooting starts. I owe him some thanks, but how do you apologize to a dragon?"

I thought about my recent discovery of Gleep's ability to talk, but a promise is a promise and I decided to keep his secret, even from Aahz.

"Just take some time and talk with him," I said. "I think he can read the tone of people's conversation, even if doesn't understand the actual words."

"Do you really think so?"

"I'm certain of it," I said, sipping from my drink. "I was just down at the stables visiting him, and I'm sure he understood what I was saying."

"At the stables, eh?" Aahz smiled. "I kind of figured that was where you were."

"Oh?"

"Well, it's where you usually go when you're upset and want to think things over."

It seemed my secret retreat was not as much of a secret as I had imagined.

"Yeah. I was upset," I said defiantly. "Even you have to admit that this time I had reason to be."

"No argument there," Aahz said with a shrug. "If anything, I'm impressed that you've recovered as quickly as you have. I notice the specific use of 'was' when you referred to your mood."

"As you say, I thought things over."

"Can I ask what you came up with?" Aahz said. "Or would that be prying?"

I took another long drink from my wine.

"Well, there are a couple things that people have pointed out to me that I've come to realize are true," I said finally. "First off, that I'm not happy. Second, that until I figure out what it will take to make me happy, I'm making myself and everybody around me more than a little crazy."

"Bravo," Aahz said, clapping his hands lightly. "Couldn't have put it better myself. Who was it that managed to get that across to you?"

"Well, General Badaxe, for one," I said, smiling slightly at the memory. "Of course, he had to kick me in the butt first, literally, to get my attention."

"Excellent." Aahz smiled. "I'll have to remember that teaching technique. Go on."

"Well, trying to sort things out, I've been fairly successful at coming up with what I don't want to do. Case in point is that I don't want to marry Queen Hemlock, and that's all the justification I need to step back from that situation. Same thing with running the kingdom if she had tried to abdicate . . . which she didn't, by the way. If I don't want to do it, I don't have to. I've been letting myself get jerked around too long by what other people want or expect me to do instead of focusing on what I want to do."

"Again, no argument," Aahz said. "Go on."

I slumped slightly in my chair.

"That's the problem," I said. "I can't seem to come up with what I *do* want to do . . . what it would take to make me happy. That's why I'm here. For a bit of sage wisdom and advice. So, talk to me, Aahz. What's the answer?"

Aahz took a sip of his own drink, then sighed and shook his head.

"Sorry, partner," he said. "I can't help you with that one."

I blinked in surprise, then saw red. All the anger and frustration I had been feeling lately came rushing to the fore, and this time, I didn't try to rein it in.

"That's it?" I snarled. "After all these years of nagging and lecturing me on stuff I didn't want to hear, when I finally come to you with a question, it's 'Sorry, I can't help you'?!"

I stood up and slammed my goblet down on the table.

"Sorry to have bothered you," I hissed.

"Sit down, Skeeve," Aahz said carefully. "We still have things to talk about."

"We'll talk later," I said coldly. "Right now, I've got to get some fresh air."

I turned and headed for the door.

"We'll talk *now*," I heard Aahz say behind me.

I kept walking, waving a dismissive hand over my shoulder.

"I SAID 'WE'LL TALK *NOW!'!!!*"

That was a tone I had never heard from Aahz before, and it stopped me in my tracks. I turned to face him.

He was on his feet, fists clenched and all his muscles taut, as if he was physically being restrained from throwing himself at me. Even his scales were a darker shade of green, and his golden eyes were positively glowing.

Looking at him, I experienced a series of flashback images, all overlaid on his current stance and posture. Aahz when he first suggested that I become his apprentice. Aahz when he discovered that I had bought Gleep. Aahz when I brought Markie home from the Dragon Poker game. The numerous times he had expressed his frustration at my ignorance and my fumbling efforts to learn magik. Aahz leaping into the path of the bug creature as it tried to trample me in the big game. The look on his face just before he agreed to leave Perv and return to Klah with me.

As fast as the images danced through my brain, my anger was dispelled.

"We'll talk now," I said, calmly.

I walked back to my chair and reseated myself.

It took a little longer for Aahz to settle down. He stood there breathing deeply for several moments, then drained his goblet and refilled it from the pitcher.

"Sorry, partner," he said, his voice still tight. "You can still get under my scales sometimes. You'd think, after all these years, I'd be used to it. I've tried to teach you as best I can, but sometimes it seems like you're determined to not listen."

"I'm listening now, Aahz," I said.

He took a long, slow breath, then blew it out completely.

"Right," he said, sitting down again. "Let's take it back to just before you blew your stack.

"I didn't say I wouldn't help you with your problem. I said I *couldn't* help you. No one can. No one can tell you what you want or what it will take to make you happy. You're the only one who can answer that question. If anyone else tries to come up with an answer for you, and you listen, then you're right back where you started . . . trying to live out someone else's interpretation of what you should do."

That made a lot of sense. It gave order to a lot of the confusion that had been haunting me.

"I can see that now," I nodded. "The trouble is, it doesn't help me much at coming up with an answer."

Aahz gave me one of his toothy smiles.

"What I can do, partner, is give you some advice."

"I'd appreciate it," I said sincerely.

He thought for a moment, then nodded, almost to himself.

"Here it is," he said. "We've pretty much wrapped things up here at Possiltum. We could head back to the Bazaar, but we're probably going to want to stick around for Massha's wedding."

He reached out and clinked his goblet against mine.

"So, here's what I suggest. Take a break. Give the whole crew a vacation . . . they could use it after this assignment. In the meantime, take some time for yourself. No work, no assignments, no pressure. Heck, even get away from the rest of us. Wander the kingdom a bit, even if you have to do it in disguise. Sit under a tree by a river. Try your hand at fishing or hunting. That will give you a lot of time to think and reflect without distractions. Then, after Massha's wedding, we'll talk again."

I thought about it. Taking a vacation certainly wasn't something I would have come up with on my own, but the more I considered it, the better it sounded. Some time with no pressures or schedules to worry me while I tried to sort things out. At the very least, it wouldn't hurt, and it might just help me make up my mind.

"That's a good idea, Aahz," I said, raising my goblet to him in a small toast. "Thank you. I think I'll give it a try. In fact, if you'll take care of passing the word to the rest of the team, I'll get started tonight."

NINETEEN

> *"How can it be a wedding without an aria?"*
> **FIGARO**

I had never been to a wedding before, so I had nothing to compare Massha's ceremony to. Several people told me, confidentially, that one would have to travel far and long to find one to top it.

Of course, as a member of the wedding party, I had a front-row seat for most of the proceedings. As the General had predicted, I had the honored role of giving Massha away. I had been away taking my vacation when most of the plans were finalized, so I was a little surprised when Big Julie appeared to take the post of Best Man.

Once my role was finished, which occurred relatively early in the ceremony, I had little to do other than stand and watch. As I mentioned, I was relatively unfamiliar with what all was going on, other than that it seemed to take much longer than I would have expected.

Apparently I wasn't the only one who felt this way, because I heard a couple others in the crowd quietly commenting on how long it was lasting. The usual answer, invariably accompanied by a smirk or chuckle, was that

it would go on until Massha sang. At the time, that didn't
make any sense to me, as, to the best of my knowledge,
there was nothing in the plans or ceremony that called for
Massha entertaining the crowd. In hindsight, it was just
as well that I was ignorant of the snide joke that was
behind the comment. If I had known then what I eventually found out, I might have taken a swing at the snick-
erers, ceremony or not. Of course, I also found out later
that, in some cultures, a scuffle or two at such ceremonies
was not only acceptable, but almost expected.

Even though I was inexperienced with such events, I
had sat in on enough of the preliminary planning sessions
that I pretty much knew what to expect from the ceremony. I was totally unprepared, however, for the reception afterward.

It was officially held in the palace courtyard, as there
was no room large enough to accommodate everyone,
though I heard that the party spilled out onto the streets
of the town as the bulk of the citizens indulged in a little
undeclared holiday. The only notable exceptions were the
caterers and tavern owners, who did a booming business
all day long.

It wasn't surprising, considering the General's long-
time standing with the military, that what seemed like a
major portion of the Army showed up to help him cele-
brate. What was a little surprising was the number of no-
tables I spotted in the crowd who I hadn't seen at the
actual ceremony.

Don Bruce, the Mob's Fairy godfather, was there along
with a small contingent of his cadre. They spent a lot of
time standing and watching the crowd, now and then hud-
dling in conversation with Guido, Nunzio, and, occasionally, Bunny.

Even Robb and his friends from Sherwood Arms were
there. We had managed to work out a deal where the
Royal Game Preserve was now a public park, and we even

managed to get a minor stipend for them as ranger/custodians. They turned out to be fairly nice people, and had taken to stopping in, off and on, to visit Gleep and bring him little treats until I began to be concerned about him getting spoiled.

Even more surprising to me was the smattering of folks from the Bazaar at Deva who showed up. Apparently, Tananda had mentioned to a few people where she was going when she temporarily closed the M.Y.T.H. Inc. office, and the word spread. I guess they had heard that, at least at this spot in the dimension, people were sort of used to seeing demons about, as they did not even bother with disguise spells. The other attendees tended to give them wide berth, but other than that there did not seem to be any panic or animosity caused by their presence. Of course, it would have been interesting to find out how many other demons were present that did use disguise spells to blend in with the crowd.

All in all, it was a festive gathering, and I found I was content to stand quietly against a wall, leisurely sipping at some wine and watching the goings-on. Occasionally someone would wander up and chat for a few moments, but for the most part I was left to the role of interested observer. The main focus of attention was elsewhere, and I was just as glad to be simply a minor player.

"It is kind of nice not to be center stage for a change, isn't it?"

I glanced over to find Queen Hemlock leaning against the wall next to me. It was a testimony to how raucous things were that she could walk around the crowd virtually unnoticed.

"Funny," I smiled. "I was just thinking much the same thing."

"It was a lovely ceremony, wasn't it?" she said. "Are you sure you don't want to change your mind? About me and you, I mean."

Not that long ago, that suggestion would have thrown me into a blind panic. As a matter of fact, not that long ago, it did. Now, however, I simply favored her with a sad smile.

"Come now, your Majesty," I said. "I think we've gone over all that before."

"I know," she said with a grin. "But you can't blame a girl for trying."

"It was a nice ceremony, though," I said. "Even though I must admit that I'm glad Massha didn't have to entertain."

"Entertain?" the Queen said, cocking her head to one side. "Whatever are you talking about?"

I explained to her the comments I had overheard during the ceremony.

"Oh, really?" she said, her voice suddenly dropping several degrees. "Do me a favor, Lord Skeeve. If you should happen to see any of those people here at the reception, would you be so good as to point them out to me?"

"Um . . . sure," I said. "But why? . . . if you don't mind my asking."

"Let's just say that I've grown very fond of Massha while we were planning this little shindig together," Queen Hemlock smiled. "Oh, by the way. I've been thinking over your idea, and the more I think about it, the more I like it."

I had made the suggestion to her that, since the M.Y.T.H. Inc. crew would be moving on soon, she might want to consider offering the post of Royal Magician to Massha.

I was about to say something in return, but she suddenly held up a hand.

"Whoops! Gotta go now," she said. "They're about to throw the bridal bouquet. Don't want to miss out on the brawl."

With that, she moved back into the crowd, not exactly running, but certainly moving faster than her normal queenly glide.

What happened next was as fascinating as it was puzzling. Massha gathered together a fair-sized crowd of young women, including Bunny, Tananda, and Queen Hemlock. Then she deliberately turned her back on them, and tossed the bouquet of flowers she had been carrying back over her head into their midst. The ensuing scramble was not for the weak of heart.

What I couldn't understand was, with all the flowers adorning the courtyard and tables, why they couldn't just each take some instead of brawling over this particular bundle.

"I've faced armies and I've faced demons," came a voice from beside me, "but I'd resign my commission before I'd voluntarily wade into that cat-fight."

"Hello, General," I said, smiling at him. "You might want to consider recruiting some of them into the Army. I'll have to agree with you . . . they're terrifying."

"If we could get them to stop fighting each other long enough to aim them at the enemy, it might be worth considering," he laughed back. "And by the way, I thought we had agreed it was 'Hugh,' not 'General,' when we talked together."

"Sorry, Hugh," I said. "Old habits are hard to break. By the way, in case it got lost in the madness, my heartiest congratulations to you both."

"And my thanks to you, Lord Skeeve," he said, giving a half bow. "We owe you much . . . as individuals, as a couple, and as a kingdom."

"I just did what I could," I shrugged. "I just wish I hadn't been so clumsy about it all."

"Actually," Hugh said, "I was referring to the last several years in their entirety. Still, I see the subject is making you uncomfortable, so I'll let it drop. Friends should not make each other uncomfortable on occasions such as these."

"As a matter of fact, I'm more comfortable than I can recall ever being before," I said. "But the thought is appreciated, anyway."

"There you are! C'mere, Hot Stuff!"

Massha had come surging out of the crowd to sweep me into a gargantuan hug.

"Oh, Skeeve," she whispered, her voice much softer than her usual boisterous self. "Thank you so much. For everything. I've never been so . . . oh, here I go again."

She hid her face on my shoulder as tears started to leak from her eyes.

Hugh looked at me over her shoulder and winked.

"Come, my dear," he said gently, putting a hand on her back. "We mustn't neglect our guests. They're expecting us to lead off the dancing."

"That's right," she said, straightening and dabbing at her eyes. "Don't go away, Skeeve. We want to share a drink with you before all this breaks up."

I watched as they made their way back into the crowd, and realized I was smiling.

They were both so happy they glowed. They had settled on what they wanted to do and then gone ahead and done it. No apologies, no trying to work it around other people's opinions.

Well, the truth of the matter was that I was happy now, too.

Aahz's suggestion had been right on the money. My vacation had given me the time I needed to straighten out my head and review my options. After all these years, I knew what I wanted to do.

Now it was just a matter of letting the team know at the M.Y.T.H. Inc. staff meeting tomorrow.

"So, when are the fireworks going to start?" a harsh voice demanded, interrupting my reverie.

I looked up to find a rather hefty young lady confronting me, hands on her hips and scowling.

"Fireworks?" I said. "I don't think anyone is going to get into a fight here . . . unless you count that melee for the flowers a few minutes ago."

"No, I mean sky-rockets and stuff," she said. "Gandalf was famous for his fireworks displays any time he attended a party."

"I don't believe I've met the gentleman," I said. "As far as sky-rockets go, however, I don't believe there are any planned."

"I guess Robb was right," she said, pursing her lips. "You really aren't much of a magician, are you?"

This lady was starting to annoy me, but, keeping with the spirit of the occasion, I tried to be polite.

"Robb?" I said, ignoring her comment about my abilities. "The gentleman from Sherwood Arms?"

"That's right," she said. "We got to talking with him at the Tiki Lounge, and he insisted that we didn't have to worry about you as a force of evil, much less do anything about you."

"That's reassuring," I said drily.

"That being the case, I guess I should give this back to you."

Fumbling with her belt pouch, she fished out a small, cloth-wrapped bundle and thrust it at me.

"What is it?" I said, deliberately not reaching for it.

"It's the ring that sort of disappeared from your room," she said with a shrug. "Finger and all. It's just a little purple from us dropping it in Volcanos."

For a change, I knew exactly what to do . . . and what not to do. What I didn't do was ask for a clarification or accept the ring.

"Actually," I said carefully, "it's not mine. It really belongs to the Queen."

"The Queen?"

"Yes. Queen Hemlock. That's her right over there," I said, pointing. "I think it would be better if you returned it to her personally. I'm sure she'll want to reward you properly."

"If you say so," she said. "Thanks for the tip."

With that, she turned on her heel and went marching off to confront the Queen.

I ran a hand across my face, hiding my smile. Yes indeed. This party was just getting better and better.

Just then, I noticed that Don Bruce was standing nearby by himself. Catching his eye, I left my wall to join him.

There were a couple of things I wanted to go over with him before tomorrow's meeting.

TWENTY

"I suppose you're all wondering why I asked you here."
D. MACARTHUR

Everyone was in attendance when I walked into the meeting.

Aahz was at his familiar perch in the window. Guido and Nunzio were holding down one end of the table, and Chumley and Tananda were seated next to them. Bunny was sitting a few chairs away, slightly apart from the rest of the group, her pad out and ready to take notes. The only one missing was Massha, but, under the circumstances, that was understandable. Besides, she had already told us she was resigning from M.Y.T.H. Inc., and this was a planning session for the future.

Prior to, and just after the wedding, I had had a chance to speak with a few of the team, but not all of them and not in detail. As such, there was an air of expectancy in the room. Everyone knew something was up, but nobody was sure exactly what.

I took the seat at the head of the table, and for a few moments just scanned the room, looking each of them in the eye one at a time.

"Any way you look at it," I said, finally, "it's been quite an assignment."

There were smiles and grimaces at that.

"What's more, it wasn't even a paid job. Oh, we eventually showed a healthy profit," I nodded pointedly at Aahz, "but, if you'll recall, it started out as a freebie. Specifically, I was worried about what Queen Hemlock was doing here in Possiltum but felt I had to travel to Perv to square things away with Aahz. Consequently, I asked the team to pinch hit for me. Again, not a job. Just a favor for me.

"Those investigations ending up being an assortment of exercises, placing everyone under stress and, in some cases, physical danger. Still, by the time we arrived here, things were pretty much in hand.

"When we got back, however, we discovered what Queen Hemlock really had in mind. Again, the whole thing with her proposal of marriage, as well as trying to straighten out the kingdom's finances, was essentially my problem. Still, the team pitched in, helping me out on all levels—including some I didn't know about at the time— and, as per usual, we fought and conned our way though it all."

There were some smiles swapped back and forth, but I noticed there were also those who were watching me carefully.

"On another level, however," I said, "this assignment has raised some questions in my mind. One of them, in particular, has been distracting me through this whole thing. It's affected my judgment and performance, and placed the rest of you in the position of having to work around me . . . or, in some instances, behind my back. That question is: What do I want?"

I glanced over at Aahz and inclined my head slightly.

"As my partner and mentor told me, that isn't a question anyone else can answer for me. It's something I had to work out for myself. So, during our break before Massha's wedding, I spent some time by myself addressing that specific question. It took a lot of thought, but I have finally come up with an answer."

I took a deep breath and thought for a moment. Now that I had arrived at my reason for calling the meeting, I found myself strangely reluctant to verbalize it.

"When I first took up with Aahz," I said, "my old magik teacher had been killed and we had a couple assassins on our trail. Practicing magik then was mostly a matter of survival.

"When that was done, Aahz kept up my lessons, but it still seemed to be one situation after another. If it wasn't a matter of helping out one of our friends, then it was following our endless quest for financial stability.

"Eventually, it evolved into what we have now: M.Y.T.H. Inc. That started out as a simple matter of pooling our talents for mutual support and improved marketing, and has become successful far beyond our initial expectations."

I paused and looked around the assemblage.

"I can't speak for the rest of you, but I, personally, have accumulated more money than I ever expected to see, and probably more than I could spend in two lifetimes. While Aahz may insist there is no such thing as enough money, I think there comes a point where accumulating more wealth becomes simply a habitual exercise rather than an actual need."

I gave a little shake of my head.

"As for the work itself, for a long time now what's been keeping me going is my own exaggerated sense of responsibility. In hindsight, it isn't really surprising. Until I took up learning and practicing magik, I was a nobody that no one depended on or looked to for help. From that start, I was catapulted into the limelight. Suddenly I could make a difference, or people expected me to make a difference, and I got caught up in being needed. Our clients needed me. The kingdom needed me. Most of all, the team needed me, and I was bound and determined not to let them down if it was at all within my power."

I gave a little laugh.

"Of course, it eventually came to light that my friends were working overtime to help me. That they would see me, in my zeal, bite off more than I could chew and would pitch in to give me moral, physical, and magikal support in whatever I had set my sights on. All in all, it's become more than a little circular.

"Well, as I said a moment ago, I've given it a lot of thought, and have decided what I want to do, what I think will make me happy. I want to study magik. Seriously. Not slap-dash picking up tidbits on the fly while we're adventuring, but conscientious, organized study.

"I've spoken with Aahz, and he's sure I can arrange for correspondence schooling from MIP, his old alma mater on Perv. What's more, I've arranged for a house here on Klah for my studies. Actually, it's an old inn and tavern where Aahz and I were holed up for a while before we hired on here in Possiltum and eventually moved to the Bazaar. It's off the beaten path, so there should be minimal distractions, but there's plenty of room if anyone drops by to visit."

I paused, and took a deep breath.

"As you've probably guessed, this will require my stepping down from being Chairman of the Board for M.Y.T.H. Inc., and retiring from being an active member of the team. It wasn't an easy decision to make; in fact, it's probably the hardest decision I've had to make in my life. Still, it's what I think will make me happiest, and I've got to give it a try. I can only hope you'll all wish me the best of luck, and stay in touch."

I paused for a moment to give it a chance to sink in.

"Now, this is supposed to be a planning session for the

directions M.Y.T.H. Inc. will go next. Obviously, my retirement will have an effect on those plans. Probably one of the first things to discuss is whether or not you want to keep the corporation going at all."

I glanced over at Guido and Nunzio.

"I had a long talk with Don Bruce at the wedding reception yesterday. While he wasn't wild about my stepping down, he's agreed to go along with whatever decisions you come up with today. M.Y.T.H. Inc. can continue to represent the Mob's interests on Deva or step back, whereupon he will try to find other representatives. As for Guido and Nunzio, whom he originally assigned to me as bodyguards, he is giving them the choice of continuing their work with M.Y.T.H. Inc. or returning to the Mob for reassignment."

I looked over at Bunny and smiled.

"I have asked Bunny to accompany me in my new endeavors as my personal secretary and assistant. She hasn't given me her answer yet, but it may be affected by how this meeting goes."

I shifted my gaze to the remaining three team members.

"Aahz, Tananda, and Chumley all had other things going for them before they met me and we eventually formed the corporation. Again, I figure it is up to them if they want to continue working with M.Y.T.H. Inc. or strike on out on their own."

I paused to collect my thoughts. This was turning out to be even harder to say than I had anticipated.

"This meeting is to discuss the future of M.Y.T.H. Inc., and since my resignation means I will not be a part of it, I feel it's only fair that I not be included in that discussion. If nothing else, there might be some things you want to say that would be hard to say in front of me.

"While I'll want to have a drink or five with all of you and say my goodbyes before I leave for my new home, right now you have a lot to discuss. As such, I guess it's time for me to excuse myself from the meeting and let you get on with business."

I started to get up, but Aahz uncoiled from his window and held up a restraining hand.

"Before you go, partner, I think we can spare a few minutes more before we start the meeting. There's something that should be said, and I guess I'm the logical person to say it."

I settled back into my chair.

Aahz stood looking at me for a moment before he spoke.

"Skeeve," he said, finally, "we've all been through a lot together over the last several years. We've fought together, bled together, drank together, and conned the customers together. We've argued and gotten upset with each other, but when the chips were down, we were always a team. You have a habit of putting yourself down, but you assembled this team. You've given it leadership, and you've given it heart. We'll respect your decision to step down, but before you leave the meeting, give us a chance to say 'Thank you' for all you've done for us."

With that, he started clapping. The rest of the team was close behind him, rising to their feet and applauding me, some smiling, some crying, but all looking at me with love and affection in their eyes.

I was both surprised and overwhelmed with a wave of emotion.

"Thank you," I managed. "Thank you all."

Blinking back tears, I got up and left, walking out of my past and into my future.

M.Y.T.H. INC. INSTRUCTIONS

First down the long white aisle came the flower girls, ten of them, dressed in green organza tossing handfuls of petals into the air. I got a faceful of their perfume and sneezed. That expression caused me to bare my teeth involuntarily, causing an equally involuntary back step by the six people standing nearest to me in the great hall of Possiltum Palace. I never expect Klahds to really appreciate Pervect teeth like mine.

I tugged at the tight collar of the formal tunic I'd let Massha talk me into wearing. If she hadn't become such a valued associate of mine and Skeeve's, I would tactfully have arranged to be elsewhere on this, her special day of days. But if you are smart, you will never say 'no' to a woman about to get married, unless you're planning on finishing the sentence with "of course I don't mind you dressing me up like an organ grinder's monkey." Which, naturally, leads your former apprentice and present partner to ask what an organ grinder is. When I explained, he said it sounds like a devious torture device—which, now that

I come to think of it, isn't all that far from being accurate, if you consider your inner ear an organ.

The horde of little girls was succeeded by a host of little boys dressed up like pages. Every one of them looked like I felt. I know Massha has a somewhat garish color sense, but I'd have done a little better for these kids than coral and pink striped satin breeches and caps, and bright aqua tunics. All around me I could see optic nerves shorting out, and the bridal attendants hadn't started down the aisle yet.

Before I'd finished the thought, here they came in a bevy. A lot of the bridesmaids were of Massha's globular body type, though none of them matched her in sheer magnificence (this *is* her wedding day. It behooves me to be more than my usual tactful self). Her confidence and warmth brought out the best in fellow large ladies of the Possiltum court, who sought her out as a friend and role model, helping them to like themselves as they were. She had plenty of friends there. Even Queen Hemlock, whom I would have voted "Girl Least Likely to Have Friends of Her Own Species," had gotten onto cordial, even warm terms with her.

In an unusual display of insecurity Massha had run color choices for the ladies' gowns past Bunny, who has a good eye for fashion. Instead of a wallow of wild hues, which is what I would have expected, the bridesmaids were all dressed in pale pink silk. In spite of the vast difference in complexions and sizes, the pink served to flatter rather than draw attention. Bunny herself looked glorious and demure in her gown. The pink even looked good against the green of Tananda's hair. She resembled some species of orchid, shapely and exotic. I'd never before seen bridesmaids' dresses that didn't look like bedspreads or horror costumes. Mentally, I awarded points to Bunny for skill and Massha for knowing when to ask for help. It just showed what kind of trust the team inspired.

Subtlety ended with the arrival of an entire marching

band. Two women in pink and aqua skirts shorter than anything Tanda had ever worn on a job catapulted into the room and began to turn flips down the white carpet. Behind them, a drum major in bright orange and blue came to a halt at the door and blew a sharp blast on a whistle. He hoisted his baton high and marched forward, leading the Possiltum army's music corps in full dress uniform, playing Honywagen's Wedding March. This was a discordant dirge that had become traditional for weddings across the dimensions, to the everlasting regret of real music lovers. Since the band was a little heavy on bagpipes and horns, the effect was as hard on the ears as their outfits were on the eyes. Since we Pervects have more sensitive ears than Klahds, I was ready to kill someone by the time they finished mauling Honywagen and struck up "A Pretty Girl is Like A Melody."

A full colorguard strode in time to the tune. The eight soldiers took positions at intervals along the white carpet, holding the Possiltum flag high. Ten more soldiers, Klahds in the peak of physical perfection, such as it is, marched in past the flag-bearers, sabers drawn and held erect in front of their noses. At a cue, they formed an arch with their swords. The band halted in the middle of its song, and struck up the Possiltum marching song. Enter Big Julie, in his best armor, clanking with weapons.

There'd been a lot of discussion about who would be the General's best man, but the former strongman turned out to be the perfect choice. After all, the traditional role of best man was to hold the door and keep unwanted visitors from intruding on the ceremony. Except for me, Guido, Chumley and a few of Don Bruce's enforcers who were present as invited guests, Big Julie was the only person who was big enough and mean enough to prevent any potential interruptions. As soon as he reached the front of the room Hugh Badaxe appeared at the door.

If there was ever a groom who wasn't nervous at his

wedding I never met him. The big man had beads of sweat on his forehead under the crest of his helmet. He ought to be nervous; he was getting a terrific wife who had a lot of dangerous friends who'd still be looking out for her well-being even after she married him. The people around me backed further away. I realized I was smiling again. Still, he bore himself with military pride. Pretty good under the circumstances.

Badaxe wasn't a young man, but neither was Massha a spring chicken. I hated wallowing in sentimentality, but it was kind of nice that they'd found each other at a comfortable time of life. I admired him for his honesty. He ran a good army. She was a terrific woman, and a decent magician, even if her power did come from gizmos. It was a good match.

As if he suddenly remembered where he was and what he was supposed to be doing, Badaxe lurched forward, then regained his composure. He walked forward with his head high, smiling at faces he recognized in the audience. I caught his eye, and he nodded to me. I nodded back, warrior to warrior, businessman to businessman. Once at the front of the room, he removed his helmet and handed it off to Big Julie.

A team of acrobats came hurtling into the room, followed by jugglers and fire-eaters. Dancers, accompanied by musicians playing zithers, harps and flutes, undulated down the white strip, flirting with guests and flicking colored scarves around like filmy rainbows. In their midst, eight pink and purple-dyed ponies drew a flatbed cart down the aisle. On it sat a tall, slender, bearded man in black leather pants and a silver tunic playing arpeggios on a tall, slender silver harp.

"Quite something, eh?" Chumley whispered. Behind me, he was leaning against a pillar so he wouldn't block anyone else's view. I nodded. Neither one of us wanted or needed to be part of the ceremony. It was busy enough without us.

There wasn't a hint of magik anywhere. Massha wanted things to go well, but she wasn't going to force them that way artificially. I thought it was pretty brave of her.

The dancers and jugglers surrounded the altar at the front of the room where a green-robed priestess was waiting with the bridesmaids and the groom.

The harp struck up the Honywagen fanfare, and all eyes turned to the door.

In my wildest dreams I could never have pictured Massha looking lovely. Radiant, perhaps, but something about the look of joy on her face transformed her from plain to fancy. The unspoken rule that crossed dimensions held true here: all brides are beautiful.

The bodice of the white silk gown could have gone around Tananda or Bunny five or six times. It was sewn with crystals, pearls and, if my eye was still good, genuine gemstones. Massha probably had a bundle leftover from her income from M.Y.T.H. Inc., and here was where she'd chosen to spend it. The skirt, which extended behind her into a train five yards long, was picked out in crystals that flashed on and off as she walked, and embroidered with little scenes in white silk thread. I'd have to get a close look at them later and find out what she thought was important enough to memorialize on her wedding dress. She'd never been one to wear shoes just for looks, but today she'd broken her own rule and splashed on crystal sandals with five-inch spike heels. Her orange hair was gathered into a loose knot underneath a wreath of pink and orange lilies and a white veil that flowed down around her shoulders. I wondered about the symbolism of all the white and thought it was quite possible she was entitled to it. Even if the color was purely for the ceremony, it looked great on her. She was like a glistening pearl as she entered on Skeeve's arm.

My partner, who often looked like a kid in spite of his years, looked grave and thoughtful, which went well with his full magician's robes. I thought it was a nice touch: since Badaxe was wearing his uniform, Skeeve, who was giving away the bride, wore his. I knew Massha and the seamstresses had been working on the outfit while Skeeve was away. The plum velvet was picked out in silver and gold constellations, magik sigils and mystic symbols which, on closer scrutiny proved to be phrases in languages from other dimensions. I particularly liked the one in Deveel near his knee that read "This space for rent." Massha squeezed his arm and he smiled up at her.

I watched them go up the aisle, master and apprentice together. It was hard to know which one was which sometimes. Skeeve seemed to be everybody's apprentice, as well as mine. He learned from everybody he met, including Massha, but sometimes, like now, he was an adult guiding someone who trusted him. He was the only person who was surprised when Massha asked him to give her away. I felt my eyes burn suspiciously.

"I'm not crying," I muttered, my teeth gritted. "This doesn't move me at all." I heard Chumley sniffle audibly behind me.

The general stepped into the aisle. Skeeve met him, shook hands, and transferred Massha's hand from his arm to the groom's. Massha kissed him. Skeeve blushed as he sat down beside the Queen with the other honored guests in the front row. Gazing at one another, the bride and groom went to stand before the altar.

"Dearly beloved," the priestess began, smiling. "We are all here to stand witness to the love of this man and this woman, who wish to become husband and wife. Marriage is a wonderful institution, but should not be entered into lightly. Let those who understand it stay quiet and let this couple learn it for themselves. Let us allow one or both of them to unburden his or her heart to you, but always remembering that it's usually the husband who doesn't understand what the wife is saying and the wife who claims the husband isn't listening to her anyhow and though you may wish to side with one or the other of them you shouldn't do that because they are blessed under Heaven and nobody's perfect; let the chips fall where they may and they will form a more perfect union in tolerance, so they'll both live to a happy old age together, and love is rare enough in this world that you should give them the benefit of the doubt; and should this union be blessed with children, their names will live on into infinity as honored ancestors and anyhow it's much more fun to spoil grand-children than children (your mileage may vary) you can remind them of this day on anniversaries for years to come, even if they don't remember which present you gave them. Do you, Hugh Badaxe, take this woman to be your wife? You do? Repeat after me: with this ring I thee wed. Do you, Massha, take this man to be your husband? You do? Repeat after me: with this ring I thee wed. By the power vested in me by the great gods all around us and the government of Possiltum I now pronounce this couple to be husband and wife for ever and ever under heaven onward into joyful eternity and beyond letanyonewhohasanyobjectionslethimspeaknoworforeverholdhispeace amen!"

"I need a drink," I told Chumley as soon as the wedding party marched out. "Several."

"Unless I'm greatly mistaken," the troll said, "there's Poconos punch in the courtyard."

"Good. If there's any left the guests can have some." I strode through the crowd, which parted like a curtain before me. The Klahds were used to our outworldly appearance by now, but it didn't mean they wanted to be close to us. That suited me just fine.

The first gulp of Poconos exploded behind my sinuses and burned down my throat like lava. I drank down two more cups of the fire-red liquid before sensation returned. I emitted a healthy belch, spitting a stream of fire three feet long.

"That's more like it," I said.

"I say!" Chumley exclaimed, his eyes watering. "I sus-

pect Little Sister had something to do with the mixing of
this."

"Tanda always could mix a good drink," I said.

There must have been three hundred people in the palace courtyard. Dancing had already started near one wall.
I could tell where the jugglers were by the gouts of fire
shooting up into the sky. Deveels and other transdimen-
sion travellers were doing small spells to the astonishment
and delight of the Klahds (and no doubt to their own
profit). Music and laughter rose over the din of people
shouting happily at one another. I took my cup and went
to stand in the reception line.

Massha and Badaxe accepted congratulations, hand-
shakes and hugs from everybody.

"Dear, I especially loved the birds singing while you
recited your vows."

"The jugglers made me remember my wedding day."

"Hey, what legs! What style! And you looked pretty,
too, babe."

Massha showed off the gaudy ring on her left hand,
and Badaxe beamed with pleasure. Don Bruce and his
enforcers were just ahead of me in line. The Fairy Godfather, dressed in a formal lilac tux that went well with
his usual violet fedora, fluttered high enough to kiss Massha on the cheek.

"You take care of her," he warned Badaxe. "Oh. I
brought a little something for you." He snapped his fingers. Two of his largest henchmen staggered toward him
with a giftwrapped box the size of a young dragon. "You
should enjoy it. If it doesn't fit, tell Skeeve. He'll let me
know." He turned to introduce the others in his retinue, a
slim, sharp-eyed man with bushy black eyebrows, and a
stocky, short man with no neck and short, wide hands
suitable for making a point without using a weapon.
"These are new associates of mine, Don deDondon and
Don Surleone."

"A pleasure," Don deDondon said, bowing over Massha's hand. Don Surleone's huge hands folded around Badaxe's. I noticed the general's face contort at the pressure. The burly man must've been incredibly strong.

The dancing and singing continued long into the night. I kept an eye on things to make sure nobody got out of line. I maintained eye contact with Big Julie, who was across the courtyard from me. He had the same idea, especially as so many people from the Bazaar kept turning up to give the happy couple their good wishes. So long as they stuck to that intention, I didn't mind.

"Hey, short, green and scaly, how about cutting a rug?" The cuddly presence that draped itself across my chest could only be Tananda. The pink dress was cut low enough on her shapely *décolletage* to cause traffic jams. I'd seen a few already.

"I appreciate the invitation, but I'm watching," I said.

"Who'd dare to cause trouble here and now?" she asked, but she was a professional. She understood my concerns. Enough of our old clientele and our present neighbors were around to spread the word across the Bazaar if something blew up and we couldn't handle it. We'd be going back there in a day or two. Fresh rumors would make that tougher than it had to be. "I'll get Chumley to watch things, too."

Noticing our tete-a-tete, Guido and Nunzio stopped by for a chat, and got my take on the situation. Skeeve was hanging out by himself. None of us wanted to bother him. He'd had enough stress the last couple of weeks, between the near-fatal accident to Gleep and acting as best man. Keeping an eye on his back was only what one partner would do for another. He needed some time to himself.

"Aahz, can I talk to you?"

I turned. The bride was there in neon and white. Her face looked worried in the torchlight. "Massha! How come you and Hugh aren't dancing?"

"I've got a little problem," she said, edging close and

putting her hand through my arm. Any time someone looked at us she beamed at them, but not convincingly. "We started opening the wedding presents, and one of them kind of blew up on us."

"What?" I bellowed. The whole crowd turned to look. I grabbed Massha and planted a kiss on her cheek. "Congratulations! You'll make a great court magician." Skeeve had let me know about Queen Hemlock's decision. I concurred that it was the best solution for both of them. That way she and Badaxe would have equal status at court. I knew I was trumping Hemlock's own announcement, but it was the most legitimate way I could think of to cover my outburst.

"Thanks, Aahz," Massha said, beaming from the teeth out. The crowd lost interest and went back to their drinks and conversation. She looked like she might burst into tears.

"Which gift?" I murmured.

"Don Bruce's."

My eyes must have started glowing, because she grabbed my arm. "Hold on, hot stuff. It's not his fault. If anything, it's ours. When we peeled off the paper there was this big box with a red button on one side. No instructions. My detector,"—she showed me the gaudy bracelet studded with orange stones on one arm—"didn't show any harmful magik inside, so we went ahead and pushed the button."

I sighed. "What happened? What was it?"

She giggled, torn between worry and amusement. "A house. A cottage, really. It's lovely. The carpets are deep enough to hide your feet, the walls are draped with silk hangings embroidered with all of Hugh's victories, and the windows are sixteen colors of leaded glass. The trouble is it's in the middle of the throne room."

It was. An otherwise good-looking, split-level cottage with a two-stall stable and a white picket fence had appeared practically on the steps of Queen Hemlock's throne. The room had been designated as the repository for wedding gifts, since security there was always tight, and no one was likely to wander in without an invitation, no matter how curious they were about Massha's china pattern.

Tananda and Chumley were on guard in the room. Tanda had taken off her elaborate headpiece. Chumley, a bow tie now undone under his furry chin, sat with his back against the doorpost. Nunzio and Guido, dapper yet businesslike in tuxedos, had arrived. They'd donned their fedoras as a sign to anyone who knew the trade that they were working. Massha's bridesmaids were clustered around a table full of presents. One of them was making a bouquet out of the ribbons. Another had a big bag full of discarded wrappings. Another had a quill and a bottle of ink, and was writing down who had given what.

"Has anyone told Skeeve yet?" I asked, taking the members of M.Y.T.H. Inc. to one side.

"No," said Massha.

"Don't," I said flatly.

"The Boss has a right to know," Guido said automatically, then looked guilty. "You got it. Mum."

"Have you tried to get it back in the box?"

"Of course," Massha said. "But the button has disappeared. So has the box."

I peered at the house. Fairytale honeymoon cottages didn't come cheap. This couldn't be construed as an insult from Don Bruce. Besides, as far as I knew, based upon updates from Tanda and Bunny, we were in good books with the Fairy Godfather. He was a careful man. He would have furnished instructions. So where were they?

"Has anyone else been in here that shouldn't have been?" I asked.

"No one," the bridesmaid with the quill said. Her name was Fulsa. She had round hazel eyes in a round, pink face. "A few people peeked in. Oh! There was a blue dragon in here for a while. I think he belongs to the Court Magician."

Gleep? I glanced at Massha.

"He just came in to sniff around the presents," she explained. "I think he felt left out, but I didn't really think he was well enough to be in the ceremony." She studied my face. "Any reason I should be worried about him?"

"I don't know," I said. But the two of us went out to the stable to make sure.

I'd never been thrilled that Skeeve had acquired a baby dragon. They live for hundreds of years, so their infancy and youth are correspondingly long. Gleep was still considered to be a very young dragon. He had a playful streak that sometimes wreaked havoc on our habitations. Skeeve believed he was a lot smarter than I did. I was reconciled to his presence, even grateful at times. He was still recovering from having stopped an arrow. The foot-wide trail through the straw on the way to his stall showed that something long and heavy had passed through there at least once.

A scaly blue mass in the corner began to snore as I entered. I went to stand by its head.

"Come on, Gleep," I said. "I know you're only pretending to be asleep. If you're as intelligent as Skeeve thinks I'm sure you understand me."

The long neck uncoiled, and the head levered up until it was eye to eye with me. "Gleep!" the dragon said brightly. I jumped back, gagging. That reptile's breath could peel paint off a wall.

"Did you take a piece of parchment from the throne room?" I asked.

Gleep cocked his head. "Gleep?"

Massha came to nestle close to the dragon. "I know you were there," she crooned, running a finger around Gleep's jowls. The dragon almost purred, enjoying the chin-rub. "Did you take something you shouldn't?"

The dragon shook his head. "Gleep!"

"Are you sure?"

"Gleep!" He nodded energetically.

Massha turned to me and shrugged. At that moment I spotted the corner of a parchment hidden under a pile of straw. I lunged for it. Gleep got in between me and it. I dodged to one side. He swung his long neck to intercept me.

"All right, lizard-breath, you asked for it, partner's pet or not." I grabbed him around the neck, just underneath his chin and held on. He writhed and struggled to get loose. I let go when Massha retrieved the paper. It was torn at one corner, where it had obviously been ripped away from a tack. Gleep tried to grab it back, but I stiff-armed him. He retired to the corner of his stall.

"It's the instructions," she said, scanning the page. " 'Choose the location you wish to site your Handy Dandy Forever After Honeymoon Cottage, then push the button.' Then below is an incantation." Massha's worried eyes met mine. "We didn't chant this! What if something terrible happens because we missed out on the verbal part of the spell? It might fall down!" She hurried out of the stable. Gleep let out a honk of alarm and scooted out after her.

"Come back here!" I said, setting off in pursuit. I was not going to let that goofy dragon upset the festivities. It was bad enough one of Massha's wedding presents had misfired.

Gleep was quicker than both of us. To the alarm of the bridesmaids, Gleep blocked the doorway of the throne room and was whipping back and forth, preventing Massha from entering. Guido and Nunzio ran over, their right hands automatically reaching into their coats.

"Grab him," I said.

"Be careful," Nunzio warned. "He's still healing. What's upset him?"

"He doesn't want Massha to read the spell that came with Don Bruce's present," I said. I stopped for a moment to think. That was how the situation appeared, now that I considered it. But that was ridiculous. "He can't read. How could he know something like that?"

Nunzio came up to lay a gentle hand on Gleep's neck. "Maybe he smelled a bad scent on the parchment," he said. "Dragons have a remarkable sense of smell."

Massha held out the paper in alarm. "Do you think its booby-trapped?"

"I don't know," I said, grabbing it from her. I started to read. My eyebrows rose until I thought they'd fly off the top of my head. "I see. Good boy, Gleep!"

"Gleep!" the dragon said, relaxing. He stuck his head under my hand and fluttered hopeful eyelids at me. I scratched behind his ears.

"What is it, hot stuff?"

I snorted. "I don't know how that dumb dragon knew, but his instincts were good. This isn't a barn-raising spell it's a barn-*razing* spell. If you'd recited it, it would have blown up the building and everyone inside!"

Massha's eyes went wide. "But why would Don Bruce want to do that?"

I scanned the page again. "I don't think he did. Look, the spell is printed in a different hand than the instructions." The swirling handwriting above was Don Bruce's. The message below, though also in lavender ink, was written by a stranger.

"How do we find out who did it?"

"With a little subterfuge," I said. "And a little dragon."

The boom that shook the castle was barely audible above the noise of the crowd and the musicians. I staggered out, supporting Massha. Her dress was torn and patched with black burns, and her hair was askew. Guido threaded his way ahead of us, making sure that Skeeve was nowhere in sight. We all agreed he shouldn't be bothered. I was pretty certain we could handle this by ourselves. He spotted Don Bruce and his two associates, boozing it up at one of the tables near the harpist. Don Bruce set down his goblet and kissed his fingers at the musician.

"Beautiful! That boy plays beautifully." Then he turned, and spotted us. "Aahz! Massha! What has happened to you?"

"The house," Massha said, playing her part. She let go of me and threw her meaty arms around the Fairy Godfather. "My husband. Oh, I can't say."

"What happened?" the don demanded.

Massha sobbed into a handkerchief. "We only just got married!"

"Are you saying that my present killed your husband?" Don Bruce demanded, drawing himself up four feet into the air.

"If the Prada pump fits," I growled, "wear it. The news will be all over the Bazaar in an hour: Don Bruce ices associates at a wedding!"

But I wasn't watching Don Bruce. I had my eye on his two associates. Surleone's heavy brows drew down over his stubby nose, but he looked concerned. Don deDondon couldn't keep the glee off his weaselly face.

"I'm good with casualties," he said, starting to rise from the bench. "I'd better go and see if I can help." Suddenly, a blue, scaly face was nose to nose with his. Gleep hissed. "Help?"

The dragon bared his teeth and flicked his tail from side to side. It was all the proof I needed that Don deDondon had had his hands on the parchment I'd had Gleep sniff, but I thrust it in front of his skinny nose.

"This your handwriting?" I asked.

"Gimme dat," said Don Surleone. He looked over the page. "Yeah, dat's his."

DeDondon threw up his hands. "No! I have nothing to do with any explosion! Call off your dragon!"

I did, but Guido and Nunzio were there flanking him, hand crossbows drawn but held low against the don's sides so they wouldn't disturb the other wedding guests. "You can clean up again, Massha. We have a confession."

"Confession?" Don Bruce demanded, fluttering madly, as Massha's bruises faded and her dress and coiffure regained their gaudy glory. "What's the deal?"

"I don't know the whole story," I said, sitting down and grabbing the pitcher of ale from the center of the table. I took a swig. Subterfuge was thirsty work. "But I can guess. New people in any organization tend to be ambitious. They want to get ahead right away. Either they find a niche to fill, or they move on. When you introduced these dons to Massha and Badaxe, their names didn't ring any bells with me. At first. Then you said they were new.

"The present you gave Massha was princely, but it also provided a heck of an opportunity to take you down, and at least a few of us with you. The box containing the house had a sheet of instructions attached to it. How easy would it be to add a booby-trap that Massha would innocently set off when she went to open your present? We trust you; she'd follow the instructions as they were written. At the very least, your reputation for doing business in an honorable fashion would be ruined. But your enemy didn't take into account you have a host of intelligent beings working for you from a number of species."

"Gleep!" the dragon interjected. He'd withdrawn to a safe distance, with his head against Nunzio's knee.

"Something with such an easy trigger mechanism wouldn't need extra incantations to operate. The additional verbiage aroused our suspicions, enabling us to figure the puzzle out in time to stave off disaster."

"Then why the costume drama?" Don Bruce asked, snatching the pitcher out of my hand and pouring himself a drink.

I grinned. "To draw out the culprit," I said. "If you and your associates were innocent you'd be concerned about the loss of life. And Don deDondon here knew about an explosion even though Massha never used the word. He was thinking about it because he'd rigged one to go off."

"But it did!" the scrawny don protested. "I felt it."

"A little subsonic vibration, courtesy of Massha's magik," I said, with a bow to her. "Nothing too difficult for a member of M.Y.T.H. Inc., which is why Don Bruce employs us to watch out for his interests in the Bazaar at Deva."

The Fairy Godfather turned as purple as his suit. He spun in the air to face the cowering don. "You wanted me to lose face in front of my valued associates? Surleone, Guido, Nunzio, please escort our former employee back to the Bazaar. I'll be along shortly." The meaty mafioso took deDondon by the arm and flicked a D-hopper out of his pocket. In a twinkling, they were gone.

Don Bruce hovered over to take Massha's hand. "I offer my sincere apologies if anything that I or my people have done to mar your wedding day in even the slightest way. I'll send someone with the counterspell to pack the house up again. I hope you and your husband have a long and happy life together. You made a beautiful bride." In a flutter of violet wings, he was gone, too.

"I'm glad that's over," I said, draining the rest of the ale. "Take that silly dragon back to the stables, and let's keep the party rolling."

Gleep's ears drooped.

"Now, Aahz," Massha said, "you owe him an apology. If it hadn't been for Gleep, the palace would have been blown sky high."

The dragon rolled huge blue eyes at me. I fought with my inner self, but at last I had to admit she was right.

"I'm sorry, Gleep," I told him. "You were a hero."

"Gleep!" the dragon exclaimed happily. His long tongue darted out and slimed my face. I jumped back, swearing.

"And no one tells Skeeve what happened here tonight!" I insisted. "None of it! Not a word!"

"Who, me?" Massha asked, innocently, as Badaxe wandered in out of the shadows, in search of his wife. She sauntered over and attached herself to his arm with a fluid langour that would have been a credit to Tanda. "In a few minutes I'll be on my honeymoon. Nighty-night, Aahz."

Who's Who and What's What in the Myth Universe*

*(Warning: There are story giveaways included in these write-ups. If you're planning to read the whole series from the start, you may want to use this as reference only.)

Aahz

Aahzmandius. Skeeve's partner/mentor and second main character of the series. A demon from Perv, making him a Perv-ect or Perv-ert, depending on who you ask. Despite the various depictions by the cover artists, Aahz is actually shorter than Skeeve, though longer in the arms. (The stocky build, no neck, green scales, pointed ears, and nasty pointed teeth they got right.) It is not his height but his sheer presence that dominates situations and makes him such a scene stealer. He lost his powers due to a joke (powder) gone bad back in *Another Fine Myth* (Book 1). Ever since, he has been overseeing Skeeve's progress at learning magik, as well as teaching him the ins and outs of dimension travel and survival. While people who have spoken with me often think his speech patterns mimic mine, he is actually patterned after my old friend and right-hand man from the Dark Horde, Bork the Indestructible, AKA George Hunt.

Ace/Berkley

The current U.S. mass-market (pocket book sized) publisher of the *Myth* series. Also published the *Thieves' World* shared-world anthologies and the *Phule* novels.

Ajax
A genuine Archer from the dimension Archiah, the dimension that invented archery. A bit long of tooth, but deadly nonetheless and an old friend of Tananda's. Part of the team that helped Aahz and Skeeve stop Big Julie's army in *Myth-Conceptions* (Book 2).

Anthony, Piers
Has absolutely nothing to do with the *Myth* novels, but is the author of the popular *Xanth* novels. If you enjoy the *Myth* books, you'll probably like his *Xanth* novels as well.

Asprin, Robert
Began writing the *Myth* novels in the late '70s and has been (sporadically) writing them ever since. Also known for (co) editing the *Thieves' World* anthologies and writing the *Phule* novels. Noted for his lengthy and tear-jerking apologies to publishers, agent/packagers, and readers for missed deadlines and late deliveries.

Ax, the
A faceless, unknown character assassin hired by jealous rivals in *Little Myth Marker* (Book 6) to discredit Skeeve.

Badaxe, Hugh (Gen.)
Commander of the Royal Army of Possiltum. A seasoned veteran who rose through the ranks, he is the consummate burly, ax-wielding warrior. Also was part of the team with Aahz and Skeeve when they entered the Big Game in *Myth-Direction* (Book 3).

Bee, "Spelling"
One of the crew who enlisted with Guido and Nunzio in *M.Y.T.H. Inc. in Action* (Book 9). A rather wimpy would-be magician, he ends up in the infantry along with everyone else. He only knows two spells: Dis-spell, and

dat-spell. Dat-spell is very much like the disguise spells used elsewhere in the *Myth* universe, and dis-spell . . . well, dispels the dat-spells.

Berfert
A salamander (exact origin unknown) and partner to Gus, the Gargoyle. Part of the team that helped Aahz and Skeeve stop Big Julie in *Myth-Conceptions* (Book 2).

Big Julie
Commander and chief strategist for the largest, most effective army to ever sweep across Klah. Unstoppable and unbeaten until they tangled with Skeeve's team in *Myth-Conceptions* (Book 2). Currently retired and living in a villa in Possiltum. Serves as an advisor to M.Y.T.H. Inc.

Brockhurst
An Imp, sometimes working as an assassin. He first appears in *Another Fine Myth* (Book 1) as part of the team that kills Garkin, then appears again in *Myth-Conceptions* (Book 2) as part of the team trying to stop Big Julie's army.

Bunny
Member of the M.Y.T.H. Inc. team, primarily serving as personal assistant to Skeeve. Was originally assigned to Skeeve as a Moll by her Uncle, Don Bruce. Has since emerged as an excellent financial manager and economics expert. Extremely curvaceous and cuddleable.

Buttercup
A war unicorn. Originally belonging to Quigley, given to Skeeve as a gift.

Cassandra
A lively bawd that Vic lines up as a blind date for Skeeve in *Sweet Myth-Tery of Life* (Book 10). This vamp is a

genuine vampire from Limbo, who takes it on herself to
show Skeeve the nightlife. [The fact that this character's
name is the same as that of the actress who plays Elvira
is purely coincidental.]

Chumley
A Troll, also a member of the M.Y.T.H. Inc. team along
with his sister, Tananda. Works under the name of Big
Crunch, at which times his manners and vocabulary deteriorate noticeably. (There is little work for educated, co-
herent trolls.) VERY large with tusks and different-sized
eyes.

D-hopper
A mechanical device used to travel between dimensions.
Roughly the size and shape of a bicycle handle. One sets
it by twisting different portions of the cylinder to align
various markings to indicate the specific dimension one
wishes to travel to.

demon
The common term for a dimension traveler. Usually applied by natives of one dimension to visitors/beings from
other dimensions.

Deva
Home dimension of the Deveels. Once ravaged by economic disaster, the Deveels used their dimension-traveling
abilities to travel to other dimensions, where they became
notorious as merchants supreme. Both their extreme trading skills and the horrifying tales of their home dimension
gave rise to numerous folklores on other dimensions.

Deva, Bazaar at
As there are too many dimensions for any single individual to travel in a lifetime, however long that might be,

there has developed a vast, 24/7 marketplace where the Deveels gather to sell and swap the wonders of the dimensions among themselves. It is said that if you can't find it at the Bazaar at Deva, it doesn't exist.

dimension
One of multiple worlds that exist simultaneously on different planes of existence. There are not many beings who are aware that these worlds/dimensions exist. There are even fewer who know how to travel between them.

Djinger
The dimension that Djins and Djeanies come from. It makes its money by hiring out its residents as short-term, limited-wish-granting magik users.

Don Bruce
The current fairy godfather for organized crime on the dimension Klah. At one point negotiated with Skeeve to exchange the Mob's interest in Big Julie's army for access to Deva. Later, after a wave of insurance frauds negated his efforts to sell protection to the Deveels, hired Skeeve to manage the Mob's interests in that same dimension. All that happens in *Hit or Myth* (Book 4), but he makes return appearances throughout the rest of the series. He is very fond of Skeeve, and has assigned him two bodyguards, Guido and Nunzio, as well as his own niece, Bunny, to serve as his Moll. Secretly hopes that Skeeve will marry Bunny and succeed him as head of the Mob.

Donning/Starblaze
The original trade (outsized, library-quality) editions of the *Myth* novels. Kelly Freas, hired as an editor to start their SF/Fantasy Starblaze line, was the only one to show an interest in publishing a humor fantasy novel.

Dragon poker
The most complicated card game in all the dimensions
and very popular with dimension-traveling gamblers. It's
basically a form of 9-Card Stud, except there are condi-
tional modifiers that change the value of a hand or card
depending on the number of players, the day of the week,
the compass point the player is seated facing, the color of
the room the game is played in, what the high card of the
winning hand was two hands ago, etc., etc. You get the
picture.

Duchess
Aahz's mother. Bankrupted the family with a series of
bad investments, causing Aahz to drop out of M.I.P. Lives
on Perv and still dreams of making a "big killing." We
meet her briefly in *Myth-Nomers and Im-Pervestions*
(Book 8).

Flie Brothers
Hyram and Shubert. Also known as Hi and Shu. Farm
boys who joined the Royal Possiltum Army at the same
time as Guido and Nunzio, as chronicled in *M.Y.T.H. Inc
in Action* (Book 9). Passable shots with crossbows.
Trained by their father and mother, Horse and Dragon
Flie.

Foglio, Phil
An insanely funny artist and long-time friend (of As-
prin's). Did the covers and interior art of the Donning/
Starblaze editions of Books 3 through 10 (also a reissue
of Book 1), as well as the adaptation of the first book
(*Another Fine Myth*) into graphic/comic format for WaRP
Graphics.

Freas, Kelly
Multiple-Hugo-winning artist, fellow Klingon, and the
original editor and artist for the Myth novels.

Frumple
A Deveel currently in residence in Klah after having been banished from Deva. Cuts a deal with Aahz and Skeeve that ultimately gets them lynched in *Another Fine Myth* (Book 1), though he makes occasional appearances in other volumes. [Face it, how many fantasy series do you know of where the two lead characters get lynched in the first book?]

Garkin
Skeeve's original magik teacher. Assassinated shortly after summoning Aahz from another dimension as a demonstration for his apprentice in *Another Fine Myth* (Book 1).

Geek, the
A Deveel gambler and bookmaker. Based at the Bazaar at Deva, he frequently comes out on the short end betting against Skeeve and the M.Y.T.H. Inc. team.

Gleep
A blue baby dragon "acquired" by Skeeve during his first visit to the Bazaar at Deva in *Another Fine Myth* (Book 1). His exact size seems to vary with the cover artist and (admittedly) the needs of the storyteller. Though he has an extremely limited vocabulary, there is more to him than meets the eye. More sentient that anyone in the team is aware, he is, perhaps, the only real stone killer in the whole crew, as evidenced by his firsthand viewpoint in *M.Y.T.H. Inc. Link* (Book 7).

Grimble, J. R.
The head accountant and Chancellor of the Exchequer for the Kingdom of Possiltum, and therefore a frequent advisor of Skeeve and his crew. Originally patterned after

one of my old bosses from my accounting days at Xerox, University Microfilms.

Guido
One of Skeeve's bodyguards, along with his cousin, Nunzio, and a full-fledged member of the M.Y.T.H. Inc. Team. Think of a couple NFL offensive linemen, only with weapons. At one point in his past, Guido had a supporting role in a production of GUYS AND DOLLS, and it has permanently affected his speech patterns.

Gus
A gargoyle (exact origins unreferenced), partner of Berfert, the salamander, and an old friend of Aahz's. Part of the crew that Skeeve uses to stop Big Julie's army in *Myth-Conceptions* (Book 2), and part of the team entered in the Big Game in *Myth-Directions* (Book 3).

Hemlock, Queen
The ruler of the kingdom of Impasse who joins her kingdom with Possiltum by marrying Rodrick in *Hit or Myth* (Book 4). Notably homicidal with the morals of an alley cat, it has long been her dream to go into real estate, Genghis Khan style. She was so much fun to write that I gave her a rematch. That starts at the end of *M.Y.T.H. Inc. Link* (Book 7) and inspires the situation the runs all the way though *Sonething M.Y.T.H. Inc.* (Book 12 . . . the one you're holding now).

Imper
Home dimension of the Imps. Both the dimension and the Imps are poor imitators of Deva and the Deveels. They try to negotiate, but can be outbartered.

Isstvan
The baddie from *Another Fine Myth* (Book 1). A renegade magician out to rule the dimensions, mainly by eliminat-

ing the competition, who are tapping into each dimension's magical energies. This is his second try at this project, having been thwarted in his first effort by the combined efforts of Aahz, Tananda, and Garkin, among others. For appearance, picture him as a demented Santa Claus. Last heard of running a hotdog stand at the Isle of Coney.

Jahk

A strange little dimension featured in *Myth-Direction* (Book 3) wherein the two leading city states, Veygus and Ta-hoe, decide who will run the dimension for the next year by having their representative teams square off in the Big Game. [If you think that's ridiculous, think of counting chads in Florida!] The little tongue-in-cheek twist here is that while the athletes themselves are huge monsters who have been bred specifically for the game for the last five hundred years, the bulk of the citizens are either vastly overweight or thin as rails.

Junebug

Another one of the "Bug Squad" that went though Basic with Guido and Nunzio in *M.Y.T.H. Inc. in Action* (Book 9). This one is a pretty-boy wannabe actor.

Kalvin

A mini, one-wish-only djin acquired by Skeeve in *Hit or Myth* (Book 4), but not actually called on until *Myth-Nomers and ImPervection* (Book 8). Billed as "the latest thing in designer djins!"

Klah

Skeeve's home dimension (making him a Klahd) and the locale for most of the novels that don't center around Deva. It is about as exciting as the Midwest without the technological advances. It does, however acknowledge magik and hires magicians.

Kow-tow
A nearly unreachable dimension populated by vegetarian cowboys and vampire cattle that figures heavily in Aahz and Skeeve's treasure hunt in *Myth-Ion Improbable* (Book 11 . . . well, 3.5, really).

Limbo
An unlisted dimension accessible through the (boarded-up) back door of the M.Y.T.H. Inc. team's headquarters at the Bazaar at Deva, as was discovered in *Myth-Ing Persons* (Book 5). Inhabited by creatures of the night, primarily vampires and werewolves, it is one of those dimensions that does not encourage tourism.

Massha
Originally encountered when she was working as the magician for Veygus on Jahk in *Myth-Directions* (Book 3), she takes an extended vacation from her position to sign on as Skeeve's apprentice in *Hit or Myth* (Book 4). As far as appearance goes, she's a show-stopper. She is EX-TREMELY large in all directions, which does not keep her from accenting her orange hair with green lipstick, leopard-skin bikini outfits, and enough jewelry to break a mule's back. Primarily a "mechanical" magician resorting to charms and gimmicks, she is also noted for having a heart that dwarfs her physical stature.

Meisha Merlin
The new hard cover and soft cover trade edition publisher for the Myth novels, having purchased (with the help of Bill Fawcett and Associates) the contract for *Myth-Ion Improbable* (Book 11) and *Something M.Y.T.H. Inc.* from Donning/Starblaze. They are also reissuing the first ten

titles in four omnibus editions. Meisha Merlin will be doing the new hard cover and soft cover trade edition Myth novels that Robert Asprin is co-authoring with Jody Lyn Nye.

M.I.P

The Magical Institute of Perv. Aahz's alma mater and the leading school for magical study on Perv.

M.Y.T.H. Inc.

Magical Young Trouble-shooting Heros. The name the crew came up with when they incorporated at the end of *Little Myth Marker* (Book 6). Okay, so it's not the greatest name out there. Still, it's the kind of thing you get when you leave decisions to a committee.

Nunzio

Cousin to Guido and his comrade in arms when it comes to bodyguarding Skeeve. Prior to working for the Mob, Nunzio worked a stint as a kindergarten teacher, making him the team member of choice to work with Gleep.

Perv

The home dimension of Aahz. Equally noted for its advanced magick, technology, and inhospitality to visitors. Described as looking like Manhattan, only cleaner. Skeeve finally gets to visit this dimension in *Myth-Nomers and Im-Pervections* (Book 8).

Phule, Willard

The main character of the best-selling *Phule* novels. (Hey! If I'm going to plug other authors' series, why not do the same with my own?)

Pookie

Cousin to Aahz, she is hired by Skeeve as a bodyguard while he is visiting Perv in *Myth-Nomers and Im-*

Pervections (Book 8). Unlike the stocky, heavyset males of Perv, she is whipcord-lean and moves like a panther. She decides to tag along when Aahz and Skeeve return to Klah to deal with Queen Hemlock.

Possiltum
The setting for most of the adventures in Klah. This was the kingdom Skeeve first worked for as Royal Magician, giving him a bit of a soft spot for seeing that things go well for it.

Potter, Harry
Does not appear at all in the *Myth* novels, having opted for a more formal education in another dimension/fantasy series.

Pratchett, Terry
Author of the *Discworld* novels, another humor/fantasy series you're sure to enjoy when you run out of Myth novels to read. (Okay. He writes other stuff as well, but it's the *Discworld* novels that get him a plug here.)

Quigley
Originally encountered as a demon hunter in *Another Fine Myth* (Book 1), he nonetheless ends up assisting Aahz and Skeeve in their campaign against Isstvan. At the end of that adventure, he decides he needs to learn more about this magik stuff, and heads off in the company of Tananda. When later seen in *Myth-Directions* (Book 3), he is working as the magician for the city state of Ta-hoe on Jahk.

"Road" movies (the)
The zany "On The Road To Singapore/Morocco/Rio/etc." movies starring Bob Hope and Bing Crosby. I was watching a festival of them on television (pre-cable) when I

started outlining and writing *Another Fine Myth* (Book 1), and have been watching them on videotape during my breaks while doing the final re-writes of this volume. To say they heavily influenced the tone and characterizations in the Myth novels is an understatement.

Rodrick the Fifth, King

As ruler of the kingdom of Possiltum, he is the first one to hire Skeeve full time as Royal Magician in *Myth-Conceptions* (Book 2) at the suggestion of Grimble and over the objections of General Badaxe. [Badaxe's opinions might have been swayed by the fact that Skeeve was being chosen to fight Big Julie's army instead of putting the money into expanding Possiltum's army.] Rodrick's reign and life come to an untimely and suspicious end shortly after marrying Queen Hemlock.

Rowling, J.K.

Has nothing to do with the *Myth* novels, but writes the Harry Potter books. (As if you needed me to tell you!)

Sen-Sen Ante Kid

The reigning Dragon Poker champion. Named for his habit/tradition of including a breath mint with his ante for the first hand of a game. Large, bald, and wrinkled. (He's had the title for a long time.)

Skeeve

The main viewpoint character for most of the *Myth* novels. Strangely enough, he has never been described in the series, giving the cover artists free rein. Picture him as a gangly teenager, whose body and energies have developed faster than his wisdom. Though normally insecure and angst-ridden, Skeeve nonetheless is fiercely loyal and over-responsible . . . and has a temper that surfaces from time to time which makes him formidable.

Smiley, Sergeant
The Drill Instructor who oversees Basic Training for
Guido and Nunzio when they enlist in Possiltum's army
in *M.Y.T.H. Inc. in Action* (Book 9).

Spyder
A rough-and-tumble female punker/street tough who is
part of the Bug Squad that Guido and Nunzio serve with
in *M.Y.T.H. Inc. in Action* (Book 9). Has aspirations of
joining the Mob after her enlistment.

Tananda
Also known as Tanda for short. (It took the movie types
who were optioning the *Myth* novels to point out to me
that "Tanda" was a cute form of "T-and-A"!) First appearing in *Another Fine Myth* (Book 1), Tananda has become one of the major characters of the series, appearing
in nearly every one of the volumes. An assassin and minor
magik-user, she is the ultimate sex kitten with green hair
and a voluptuous body. Much to Skeeve's disappointment,
she has adopted a "big sister" attitude toward our hero.

Trollia
Home dimension of Tananda and Chumley. Though we
never visit this dimension in the novels, it is clear that the
men are Trolls and the women are Trollops.

Vic
A young (Skeeve's age) vampire from Limbo. First seen
in *Myth-Ing Persons* (Book 5), he is currently residing at
the Bazaar at Deva, trying to break into the magik business.

Vilhelm
Makes a brief appearance in *Myth-Ing Persons* (Book 5)
as the dispatcher of Nightmares in Limbo. Based loosely

on long-time friend and hard-working packager Bill Fawcett of Bill Fawcett and Associates.

WaRP Graphics
The publishing house of Wendi and Richard Pini, best known for the *ElfQuest* saga. Coincidentally, they also published the graphic adaptations of the first two *Myth* novels.

Weasel
One of Guido and Nunzio's old associates from the Mob. Whereas they are large kneecappers who only resort to violence when the other side is too dumb to take the hint, Weasel is a thin, wiry knife-man who likes his work.

Woof Riders, The
Idnew and Drachir (which are Wendi and Richard spelled backwards), a husband and wife artist/writer team that help Skeeve in *Myth-Ing Persons* (Book 5). [And they ask writers where they get their ideas!]

Zoorik
Where the gnomes come from.

ABOUT THE AUTHOR

Robert (Lynn) Asprin was born in 1946. While he has
written some stand-alone novels such as *Cold Cash War,
Tambu, The Bug Wars*, and also the Duncan and Mallory
illustrated stories, Bob is best known for his series: The
Myth Adventures of Aahz and Skeeve; the *Phule* novels;
and, more recently, the *Time Scout* novels written with
Linda Evans. He also edited the groundbreaking *Thieves'
World* anthologies with Lynn Abbey. His most recent col-
laboration is *License Invoked* written with Jody Lynn Nye.
It is set in the French Quarter, New Orleans, where he
currently lives.